I0594295

NOT QUITE A LADY

THE BOSTON HEIRESSES BOOK 3

AVA ROSE

CONTENTS

Not Quite a Lady (The Boston Heiresses)
© Copyright 2020 Ava Rose
All rights reserved

ISBN-13: 978-0-6484045-5-2
First Print Edition
Published by Flourish Books

This book is a work of fiction. Any names, characters, places and events portrayed in this work are products of the author's imagination or are used fictitiously. Any resemblance to actual events, places or persons, living or dead, is coincidental. No part of this book may be used or reproduced in any form whatsoever in any country whatsoever without the express written permission of the publisher, except in the case of brief quotations embodied in reviews.

CHAPTER ONE

LA ROBE DORÉE, BOSTON

November, 1891

Lady Sarah Smith-Jones was utterly convinced that genteel poverty was not as romantic as books made it out to be. In literature, a wealthy lord usually marched into the stranded lady's life and offered her riches as well as his heart, after fate had subjected her to a series of tests to determine her worthiness of such a boon, of course. In Sarah's case, fate subjected her to the tests—quite often, in fact. But unfortunately, the boon was yet to appear.

So, here she was, toiling the evening away in poor lighting, as she did most evenings, to provide for her family. That should have been her father's role, but he had left her and her sisters to fend for themselves. No, the man had not packed his bags and snuck out in the middle of the night like a cad. He had done something far worse; an act of selfishness that Sarah had great difficulty understanding and forgiving. He had gambled away the family fortune, and then taken his own life.

She was only twenty-four. Ladies of her age mostly had far less complicated lives, here in Boston. She and her sisters had not even been allowed to finish grieving before the bank had taken their home. Their Aunt Bernice had grudgingly offered to shelter them for a year while Sarah searched for a way to get the family out of their dire straits, although living with their aunt had been rather difficult, as she had made Sarah and her sisters feel as if they were a burden.

A talent for sewing had led to Sarah reaching out to some of her friends for patronage, which had eventually enabled she and her sisters to move out of Aunt Bernice's home to a small townhouse in South End.

Her dressmaking shop, *La Robe Dorée,* was an endeavor of which she was inordinately proud. The name was French for The Golden Dress, and since opening the premises she had built up the business herself, on hard work and perseverance. She had the calluses on her fingers to prove it.

Sarah glanced at the clock on the fireplace mantle and released a breath. It was past five and she was running late for dinner with her sisters and Mr. Campbell, but she couldn't leave before this particular dress was complete.

More than half of the money she made went into

paying off the debts her father had saddled the family with, and what she would earn from this dress would complete a debt payment that had been hanging over her head for two years.

Only the finishing touches were left, and she was determined to see to them herself. Lady Dianne Belleville was getting married to Lord Remington and Sarah had snagged the prize of designing the bride's wedding dress. The final fitting was scheduled for the morrow, so there was no choice but to finish everything tonight before she left the shop.

"Camilla, pass me the final lace flower," she said, her eyes still on the dress neckline. Instead of finishing the edge with lace strips, Sarah had hand-cut the flowers from the finest lace in her collection, and painstakingly sewed them around the edge of the neckline with little pearls at their centers. The effect was rather pleasing.

Her assistant, Camilla, handed her the last ivory lace flower and she ran her threaded needle through it, attaching it to the dress. When she was done, she stepped away from the mannequin and regarded her handiwork. She tried to look first with a critical eye, then imagine what it might look like to a stranger. This technique helped her view things from different perspectives, and had proven most beneficial for dress commissions.

"What do you think, Camilla?" Sarah asked, placing her hands on her hips. "I do believe we have done a rather nice job of it."

“This is the loveliest dress you’ve ever made,” Camilla replied.

A knock sounded at the door and Sarah frowned. Once the hour of five had struck, Camilla had flipped the card on the door to indicate that the premises was now closed for the day. They were not expecting deliveries at this time of the evening.

So why was someone knocking now? Who could it be?

Sarah pulled back the heavy velvet curtain covering the shop window that looked out onto the street. Her heart flip-flopped in her chest at the sight of the man standing outside in the fog and drizzling rain.

Camilla gasped when she saw the man and turned to her mistress. "He looks a little…mysterious. What should we do?"

Mysterious, indeed. Sarah had half a mind to refuse to open the door to this particular caller. After all, why should she? The man had never meant any good and she suspected he was here to cause more grief. But she could not avoid him forever.

Straightening her shoulders and clenching her jaw, she said with as much calmness as she could muster—calmness she did not feel inside—"Open the door, Camilla. Let him in."

When her assistant complied, a man dressed all in black stepped in. He dwarfed everything in the room and his top hat gave him an air of regality that she knew was misleading in this case.

"It's all right, Camilla,” she said. “You can finish up

for the day."

Camilla shot a nervous look at their visitor. "Are you sure…"

"I will be fine. You may leave now."

Her assistant curtsied. "Yes, my Lady."

Sarah watched the girl head toward the back of the premises. When she heard the door at the back of the shop close, indicating Camilla's exit, she turned and confronted the tall man before her.

"Come to take my soul?" she asked, her body rigid and her jaw clenched tight.

He chuckled darkly. "Not quite yet."

"Then will you at least take off the hat?" Sarah did not like feeling intimidated.

"As you wish, my Lady," he murmured, as he lifted the damp hat from his head and ran a hand through the midnight-colored hair.

The locks were as dark as a raven's feather and his eyes as green as the brightest emerald—just the way she remembered. Unfortunately, this man's effect on her was equally familiar. She willed her heartbeat to slow down. He did not deserve any reaction from her, other than disdain.

Known as the Raven, he had a reputation as one of the wealthiest and most dangerous men in Boston. He also happened to be the one to whom her father had owed his biggest gambling debt. Since that debt had been transferred to Sarah as the eldest of Lord Smith-Jones' children, this was the man to whom she owed almost everything.

Lord Smith-Jones, Earl Waelcombe, had many debts. Sarah had paid all the smaller ones and her earnings from Lady Dianne Belleville's wedding dress would put an end to all but one. The final debt, and the biggest of all, which was held by the Raven. Sarah had yet to start paying that one.

"I don't have your money, if that is what you are here for."

"Hmm." That was the only sound to emanate from him. He set a cane with an ornate silver handle against the wall, and then removed his rain-dampened coat and hung it on a rack near the door before advancing properly into the room.

Despite her resolve not to show a reaction, Sarah took a small step back, even though he was a full three yards away from her.

"Running, are we?" he drawled.

She raised her gaze up to meet his, and lifted her chin. “Certainly not,” she said. “You found me here, did you not? I have no reason to run from you."

His mouth tilted upward at one corner. It almost looked like a sneer, and reinforced her dislike of him. "I like what you've done with this place," he said non-committally.

She lifted her shoulders in a shrug. Two could play at non-committal.

"It looks very different from how it looked last time I was here," he added.

"The last time you were here was two years ago and a lot has changed since then."

“Hmm,” he said again, wandering casually around the room as though he was inspecting it for purchase. He studied the dress on the mannequin and fingered the lace flowers she had just finished sewing onto the neckline.

"Dianne Belleville's dress, I presume." The Raven turned and raised a brow at her, his eyes keen and his expression masked.

"Yes," she replied. *What did he want?*

He was the one person she found consistently difficult to read.

"How ever did you manage to snag such a deal?" The sardonic tone made Sarah want to throw something at him. She would not give him the satisfaction of seeing how much he annoyed her, no matter how belittling his remarks.

"In much the same manner you managed to own Boston's finest gentlemen's club," she answered. “Sheer will. Plus, I might add, a great deal of skill.”

Where he'd needled her, she'd graciously complimented him. However, much she disliked the man, she had to acknowledge his ambition and what he'd achieved from the wrong side of the blanket.

"Oh, I didn't mean it as a slight. Lady Dianne Belleville wanted that French designer, Madame Fouché, or so I've heard. How did you end up taking the contract from her?" He was not looking at her as he spoke, but rather, studied the dress most intently.

She decided to answer honestly. "I offered better design options. Newer fashion."

He chuckled and stepped away from the dress. "It's an impressive talent."

She didn't bother to acknowledge his compliment of her craft. She didn't need his approval. "What do you want, Raven?"

His expression darkened momentarily. "Ever an impatient woman. You haven't changed one bit, Sarah."

"It is still *Lady* Sarah. I'm still the Earl's daughter, even if he is now the late Earl."

"Ah, you get to call me Raven, even knowing my true name, and I don't get to return the favor?"

"I'm merely addressing you by the name you gave yourself." She shrugged again. Outwardly she looked as unaffected as could be—at least she hoped so. But inwardly, she was anxious to learn of what he had come for, and even more anxious for him to leave.

"Actually, I didn't give myself that name," he corrected as he lowered himself onto a rose damask settee by the wall and stretched his long legs before him, crossing them at the ankles.

He took up a great deal of the space in the room. Sarah felt faintly claustrophobic.

"But you allowed it and lost your real name along the way."

His keen eyes focused on her then and the fine hairs on her arms stood alert. She could hear her own raspy breathing as his graze trapped her, sapping her resolve to stand up to him. He knew how to disarm her, with just a stare.

"Enough about my name. I want you to do something for me."

The Raven's words pulled her from her trance. "You want *me* to do you something for *you*?"

"Don't sound so surprised," he drawled.

"You can't just come into my shop and start demanding things."

"You've not even heard what I want you to do for me." His voice was unfeeling and he looked suddenly bored.

"I don't care what you want me to do. It's not going to happen." She waved in the direction of the door, indicating that he could show himself out.

He didn't budge. He did not even dignify her comment with an acknowledgment as he picked invisible lint from his trousers. At length, he said. "I'm sure I don't have to remind you of what you owe me."

Sarah was rendered almost speechless. Almost. "So you want to collect that payment—or part thereof—by asking me to be your lackey?"

He shrugged. "I don't see you paying off the debt any other way."

"I am trying. This dress will finalize one debt." She pointed to the dress on the mannequin. "Yours is next. You do see I'm trying, don't you?" She hated the pathetic sound of her own words.

A dark brow rose slowly. Was he mocking her? *The cur.*

"Sarah—"

"You don't have leave to use my Christian name."

"*Lady* Sarah," he amended, making her title sound more like an insult than a form of respect. "I do not see that you have a choice."

"Like hell I don't." She let go of all proper speech. She would not be manipulated by him. “I do not know what you want, but given your reputation, it can’t be anything good!”

This debt had been her father's to bear, but by the sheer cruelty of fate, it had fallen upon her. That did not mean she would allow him to drag her into his dark world in order to pay it off.

The Raven straightened to his full height and his expression shadowed. Sarah's heart leapt to her throat. He might have a reputation as a dangerous man but he wouldn't hurt a lady... would he?

"You can't refuse this offer," he said quietly. “If you do, I will call in the debt. In full.”

Sarah’s heart rate was so high she wondered if she might have a fainting spell. She took a deep breath and released it slowly. At length, she felt able to speak. "What is the offer exactly?"

"I need you to track someone down for me. They have something I want."

"Shouldn't you hire a private detective to do that for you?"

"I require a great deal of discretion."

“And a detective cannot provide that?” She placed her hands on her hips as she tried to understand why he had come to *her*.

“No.”

She shook her head. "Detective DeHavillend is the best in Boston—"

"DeHavillend is not interested, and I do not want any other detective involved, Lady Sarah." He cut her off brusquely, but Sarah was not discouraged. She would try to dissuade him from making her do this.

"You could have the police do it for you *and* keep things discreet. You and I both know you just need to choose the *right* police officer, and pay them well."

The Raven smiled cynically. "If the police were any use, your Baroness friend would not have come to you for information." His expression hardened then. "Which brings us to the subject of the information you gave her."

Sarah swallowed as the realization of what this might be about finally crystallized.

Roughly two months ago, one of her dearest friends, Her Royal Highness Elizabeth Armstrong-Leeds, Baroness Esk, had been kidnapped and forced to marry her abductor. Libby's dearest friend, Anna Trevallyn, Duchess Wrexford, and Libby's brother Penforth, together had rescued Libby after some days. Unfortunately, her abductor Mr. Nolan Hart had been found dead shortly after her rescue and Libby had become a suspect in the man's murder. Libby had come to Sarah seeking information, in the knowledge that Sarah's clothing design business allowed her access to many layers of Boston society.

Sarah might still be the daughter of an Earl and have one leg in high society thanks to her birth, but her other leg was firmly anchored in the common world thanks to her family's debasement after her father's self-destruction. Sarah was often privy to information she would not have had access to had she exclusively been in one social class or the other.

At the time of Mr. Hart's death, there had been a rumor that the Raven had ordered the assassination of Mr. Hart and Sarah had provided that information to Libby.

Now, Libby had thankfully solved her case and cleared her name with Detective DeHavillend's help. And their association had led to an unexpected matching, for they were now engaged to be married.

Sarah was delighted for her friend, but now she would have to face the consequences, because by spreading that rumor about the Raven, she had inadvertently accused him of a murder he had not committed.

"I didn't make up the rumor if that is what you're thinking," she said, not quite looking at him.

"Oh, I know you didn't make it up, but you did pass it along, without checking to see if it was true."

He was correct, and she felt bad for that, but it had helped Libby in the end. "I don't regret the fact that it did help my friend solve the case and clear her name."

"Of course," he snorted. "And your loyalty is to her."

"Would you rather I remained silent when I had information that could have helped her?"

"You didn't have information, you had a lie." The coldness in his voice sent chills through her entire body and she almost hugged her arms about herself. She stopped the action, unwilling to expose any vulnerability.

"A lie I thought was true."

For an infinitesimally small moment, she thought she saw hurt flash in his eyes, but it was gone before she could examine it. She dismissed it as fancy, because a man like the Raven could not be hurt by someone like her. Besides, he already had a tarnished image. Her piece of information would have made no difference to that.

One corner of his mouth quirked upward. "Mrs. Hart."

She waited for him to say more but he didn't. Did he want her to track down Mrs. Hart? The woman was Mr. Nolan Hart's real wife. The discovery that the man already had a wife had been a great relief for it had rendered Libby's marriage to him null and void. But Mrs. Hart was the true murderer, and she was now on the run. Like Libby, she had been tricked by Mr. Hart into marrying him and he had quickly squandered her fortune.

The woman was clearly out of her mind, and tracking her down could prove very dangerous.

"What do you want with her?" Sarah asked.

"She has something I need..." He paused as though considering his next words. "And she made up that allegation."

"Then why are you confronting me about the allegation?"

"*You* should have known better," he admonished in a voice so low it was almost a whisper.

Sarah flinched and looked away, not wanting to be reminded of their past. But it was too late. It had been two years but the pain was still raw. How could she ever forget that which had rendered her heart frozen?

"What is it that she has?" she asked after she had regained her bearing.

"Something of great value to me."

"I don't have time for riddles, Raven. Just tell me what you want from her."

"Very well. There is a ruby necklace in her possession which does not truly belong to her. Your Baroness friend and Detective DeHavillend tracked it down but unfortunately, they let the murderer run off with it."

Sarah remembered Libby telling her the tale of how they had found the necklace in their search for clues.

“Didn’t Mrs. Hart claim it was hers?”

“She may have, but she lied. The necklace belonged to Regina Ghyslaine Arbusson, my maternal grandmother, who passed it down to me. Several months ago, it was taken from a safe in my office in The Barbican.”

Sarah’s breath caught in her throat. The Raven was many things, but in her experience he was not a liar. If he claimed the necklace belonged to him, then it truly belonged to him. But Sarah was still unsure if she wanted to become involved. She quite liked her peaceful existence despite the toil that came with it. Her sisters were safe. Following the Raven would take her into a dark unfamiliar world and she could endanger everything she had worked so hard to build.

On the other hand…

"Will my father's debt to you be repaid, if I do this?"

He nodded. "Your debt will be repaid." His mouth curved in that sardonic manner of his before he added, "All of it."

She felt her eyes widen. "E-everything?"

"Yes. The book will be wiped clean. Like your family never owed me anything."

Her hands shook and she quickly clasped them. One part of her wanted to accept his offer. She and her sisters would be free and their life would improve. But the other part of her was vehemently opposed. She was torn.

This was not a decision she could make lightly.

"Give me some time," she said. "I need to think about this."

A frown darkened his handsome features. "Why do you need time? You *do* want to settle the debt, don't you?"

"I have the right to decide how I want to pay it."

"Fine." He made for the door. "You have three days." He shrugged on his coat and picked up his hat and cane.

Without another word, he opened the door and stepped out into the rain.

CHAPTER TWO

THE BARBICAN

That Evening

Tamworth Arbusson prided himself on his patience but every time he had to deal with Sarah Smith-Jones, he found that patience fraying. Today, she had given him a headache, literally.

And he had almost lost his carefully constructed composure.

Her request for time to think about his offer did not make any sense. He had expected her to jump at the opportunity because it would take a very long time for her to repay him—her entire life, most likely—unless she married a wealthy gentleman, one generous enough to pay off her debt.

Being on the receiving end of her sharp tongue was

not the reason Tam had almost lost grip on his composure. He had not seen Sarah up close nor spoken to her in over two years. Nothing about her had changed. If anything, she was even more striking; those magnetic gray eyes, that stubborn mouth…

"Sir?" The Barbican's steward, Mr. McGuire, called for his attention.

Tam looked at the man and raised an inquiring brow.

"Detective DeHavillend is here."

"Let him in."

Mr. McGuire nodded slightly and left the office. A moment later, Viscount DeHavillend walked in.

"Good evening, Detective," Tam greeted as his visitor sat in one of the chairs in front of Tam's massive mahogany desk.

"Evening, Arbusson," DeHavillend returned, placing a file on the table and pushing it toward him. "The information you requested."

Tam pulled the file to him and opened it. Therein was everything the detective knew about Mrs. Hart. "Are you sure you don't want to accept my offer?" he asked.

DeHavillend shook his head. "I do not. It is now in the hands of the police. I want no further involvement."

Tam had offered to hire the detective to track down Mrs. Hart. It was an attractive offer and he'd thought DeHavillend would accept given his previous involvement in the case, but the man had politely declined. Previously, DeHavillend would not have turned down such a case. Tam suspected it was because he wanted to protect the baroness to whom he was now engaged.

"I don't believe I have offered you my felicitations," Tam murmured.

The detective smiled and inclined his head. "Thank you." Then he rose from his chair and straightened his vest. "Good night, Arbusson."

"Good night, DeHavillend."

After the detective had left, Tam went through the file carefully, wanting to learn as much as he could about the woman. She had last been seen leaving town with two men. Protectors, most likely. She never moved unprotected.

Tamworth rose and strode to the bell near the door to ring for Mr. McGuire. While he waited, he stared out the window at the street below.

"Where is Nate?" he asked the steward without turning around as soon as he heard noise in the doorway.

"I will fetch him."

Tam returned his attention to the street. Glitzy carriages lined the road with gentlemen alighting, by the minute, to enter the Barbican. He grinned, not only at the patronage but at how far he had come in life.

As the bastard son of a duke, he had started life without a father, or any male figure worth looking up to or from whom to learn the ways of the world. But he had learned quite a bit from his grandmother, Regina Arbusson, in the little time he spent with her. His mother, Lisette, had been courted by a French marquess —now duke—and abandoned for a woman from a wealthier family. She had given birth to Tam in secret to save what had remained of her reputation, handed him over to Regina, and run off to marry an English baron, shirking all of her bonds and responsibilities.

When he was three, Tam's grandmother had moved to Boston with him in tow and they had taken up residence with his mother's brother. The sea journey had made them ill, according to Regina, but she had been happy to leave France and start afresh in a new land. She had wanted to give Tamworth a life in a place where his birth would be less likely to hinder his opportunities.

In thirty-two years, Lisette had written only once. That missive had been in response to his Uncle Laurent about Regina's death. She had not even had the decency to inquire after Tam. It had been as though he did not exist.

Tam closed his eyes briefly as the memories assailed him. Regina had meant everything to him, and when she lost her life in a horse-riding accident when he was six years old, something in him had followed her.

He had lived with Laurent for another seven years before deciding he needed to stop being a burden and make his own way. He survived on the streets of Boston by taking whatever small job came his way. He had built his wealth on toil, and some jewels that Regina had left him, but mostly toil.

These days, several gentlemen's clubs in Boston

belonged to him and the finest, the Barbican, was his favorite. Looking at the crowd below, it seemed this place was a favorite of many. There was another not-so-noble means of income: gambling. Tam did not gamble —although he was excellent at most card games—but he offered games in each of his establishments and his members were always eager to play.

He had seen many men lose their livelihood to gambling and he'd once been confronted by Sarah about it.

"Gambling is like an ailment, so why do you allow it?" she had asked, outraged when he revealed what her father had owed him.

"It's business," he replied. "It is not my fault that those who lose have no discipline."

Sarah had looked at him as though he was a monster. "And you cannot forgive even when a man is dead?"

"Took his own life," he corrected. She was referring to her father. "He wanted to force my hand. Make me forget the debt he owes me."

She shook her head, her eyes filled with hurt. "That's not true." Her tone implied she was trying to convince herself of that as much as him. "And why should *I* have to be the one to pay? The debt is not mine."

"It is the way of things. The debt *is* yours, now, as the eldest child. Especially as your cousin will not honor it." He had felt immense pity for her, but a debt was a debt and he could not let it go.

He had been tempted, but there were some that

would construe that one act as a pass for them to do what Lord Smith-Jones had done, thinking that a debt could be forgiven in the event of their death.

It was unfortunate, but Sarah would have to pay for her father's bad decisions.

"It's sad that we don't get to choose our parents," he had said softly, hoping that would ease some of her pain.

But it hadn't. She had called him a vile monster among other unsavory names.

Tam often wondered if he truly was all the things she'd accused him of being…

Nate's heavy footsteps pulled him out of his grim recollection and he turned from the window as the man walked in. He was a heavily built fellow to whom Tam accorded more respect than most. Nate was loyal and strong. He did not ask questions. And in a way, he and Tam had changed each other's lives.

Several years ago, one of his debtors had invited him to meet at the docks to receive payment. Instead of finding the debtor, he'd encountered Nate who had been sent to kill him. The two men had fought and wounded each other, and although Tam had the opportunity to finish the task, he had spared Nate's life. He discovered that the hired killer had been desperately in need of money, and Tam had offered to hire him. The two men had developed something that could almost be called a friendship, and Nate had worked for Tam ever since.

Tam moved to his desk and picked up a paper that he'd removed earlier from the file DeHavillend had brought and handed it to Nate.

"See what you can find out about her location in the morning."

Nate nodded and left. He rarely asked questions, as a matter of fact. He only spoke when necessary, and that worked well for them both.

A short while later, Tam retrieved his coat and hat and made his way downstairs. He usually left the club after ten in the evening, but it was almost midnight now.

Earlier that evening

SARAH RUSHED HOME TO THE SMALL HOUSE SHE SHARED with her sisters in South End and Millicent met her at the door as soon as she entered.

"You're late!" Millie complained, pulling her toward the drawing room.

"I was delayed by... someone unexpected," Sarah explained. Then pulled her arm from her sister's grasp. "At least allow me a moment to remove this wet wrap." She removed the cloak and handed it to their butler, Cooper.

After her father's death, Sarah had let go all the servants and only Cooper and the housekeeper, Mrs. Fowler, remained.

"A customer?" Millie asked, taking her arm again.

"No, someone else."

The curious girl ignored her dismissive tone and prodded, "Who?"

"Not now, Millie." Sarah kept her sisters abreast of everything happening in their lives. She did not believe in keeping things from them to protect them. The world could be a cruel place and the more they knew, the better prepared they would be to face whatever might eventuate.

"Well, do come on. He's here."

Sarah allowed her sister to pull her to the drawing room where a man was waiting. When they entered, he rose to his feet and bowed respectfully.

He was Jace Campbell, a gentleman with a respectable fortune and Millicent's suitor. They were having dinner with him tonight, after which he had something to talk to Sarah about, according to Millie.

It must be about marriage. What else could it be?

"Welcome, Mr. Campbell," Sarah greeted, with a smile on her face. A smile she was not feeling deep inside.

"Call me Jace, please."

She nodded and went to sit in the chair closest to the fire. The winter chills had begun to creep in and it was cold outside.

"I trust your day was good," Jace began.

She wouldn't exactly say her day was good. It *had* started off rather well, but she had grown weary as the day advanced, and the Raven's unexpected visit had taken away whatever positive effect the day had previously held. "It was quite well, thank you," she replied.

"My day was good too, and even better now that I

am here." He gazed admiringly at Millie who blushed and tugged at a curl of blonde hair that had fallen over her right shoulder.

He cared for her sister, no doubt, but Sarah would only agree to their union if Millie wanted it. His fortune could encourage her to accept him, but she was not that kind of person. No matter how poor they were, she would never force her sister to marry for money.

"And how is your family, Jace?" she asked.

"They are fine and they send their best. I was hoping we could all have dinner together sometime soon."

He had two sisters and one brother under his care and, like Sarah and Millie, both of Jace's parents were dead.

"That sounds nice. We would be happy to have a meal with your family."

"Dinner is served," Cooper announced.

Sarah led the way while Jace took Millie's arm to escort her to the dining room. On their way, Sarah realized she had not seen her sister Arabella.

"Where's Bella?" she asked Millie.

"I left her upstairs. Cooper said he would fetch her."

Bella was already seated when they arrived at the dining room. She beamed when she saw Sarah.

"Can we start eating soon? I am famished."

Sarah smiled at that. She knew the twelve-year-old had only refrained from eating because they had a guest. She would never wait otherwise.

Jace pulled out a chair for Millie before settling in his own after Sarah. Soup was served and they began to eat.

"Oh, hello, Jace," Bella greeted when she was halfway through her soup. "Forgive me for not greeting you earlier. I was just very hungry."

"You shouldn't apologize for that. Hunger is a natural thing." He smiled gently at her.

She turned to Millie with an impertinent set of her chin. "Did you hear that? I shouldn't apologize for things I've done while hungry."

"That does not include being rude and immature, Bella," Millie returned calmly.

"I am twelve years old. I still have some time before maturity is expected of me."

Millie obviously could not think of a rejoinder fast enough and so, by the law of banter, Bella won. And she wore a smirk to show her satisfaction. Sarah smiled at that. Bella knew how to turn most situations to her advantage and it was admirable.

"Do you play chess, Jace?" Bella asked.

"I play quite well," he replied.

"Would you like to go up against me?"

Jace finished the rest of his soup and put down his spoon. "Of course. It should be an entertaining match. A twenty-five-year-old man versus a twelve-year-old."

She grinned. "So, it will be quite the defeat if I beat a man more than twice my age."

He laughed and Sarah thought he fit into her family rather well.

"Have you finished the dress, Sarah?" Millie asked, as the main course was served; Pommes Anna with roast chicken and vegetables.

It was a modest meal by the standards of the upper class, but Sarah would not go beyond her means to impress anyone, not even her sister's suitor. If he couldn't accept them as they were, then Millie should not be marrying him.

"Yes, we finished it this evening. The final fitting will be in the morning and by evening the adjustments, if any, should be done."

"That is Lady Dianne's dress, is it not?" Jace asked.

"Yes, it is."

"It is all Penelope and Scarlett are talking about. They're dying to see the dress."

"I've only been able to work on the dress when there are no customers around. And whenever someone does come into the shop, they cast furtive glances around looking for it."

"The dress is getting quite the attention. One: because it's Lady Dianne. And two: because you're designing it," Millie said, with a glint of pride in her eyes. "No one expected Lady Dianne to reject Madame Fouché and hire you."

"Can we see the dress, Sarah?" Bella asked.

Sarah shook her head. "I'm sorry, but I'm under contract to keep it hidden. You'll see it on the wedding day."

"Will we be attending the wedding?" Bella asked.

"Yes, we have an invitation."

"Oh, wonderful!" Bella sighed dreamily. "I love weddings and I cannot wait for Millie and Jace's."

"Bella!" Sarah and Millie warned in unison.

Jace laughed. "Oh, it's quite all right. Please don't caution her on my account."

Sarah smiled stiffly at Jace while she gave Bella a warning look.

And she suddenly thought of their mother, who would likely have reacted in much the same manner as Sarah, had she still been here. She died when Bella was born.

"Will you be attending tomorrow's engagement ball?" Jace asked.

"Yes, I believe we will," Sarah answered.

"I will be there, too. Shall I accompany the three of you?"

She nodded with a small smile, understanding his seriousness about her sister.

When dinner was over, Sarah sat in her study with Jace in front of the fire. She was playing the role of both mother and father, especially a father, in this case.

"You already know what I want to talk to you about."

Sarah nodded.

"I want to ask your permission to make Millicent my wife."

He could have gone to their cousin to whom the title now belonged, for legally, he was Millie and Bella's guardian. The fact that Jace had come to her first, according her much respect, was a plus in Sarah's eyes.

Sometimes she felt as though the universe was against her and her sisters, and sometimes, she felt as though it was extending a hand of mercy. This moment, it seemed like the latter.

She released a slow breath and met Jace's blue gaze. He was a handsome enough man and from what she knew of his character, he would take good care of Millie. Sarah wanted Millie to be happy. Heaven knew her sisters deserved happiness and a secure future, and if she could not truly give it to them, then she had to make sure they each found someone who could.

"You have my blessing, Jace," she declared.

A gasp reached her ears from outside the study. The door was ajar for propriety and she saw dancing shadows, from her sisters, no doubt. "You can come in if you like," she called.

Bella was the first to show with pinkened cheeks and a gleam of excitement in her blue eyes. Then Millie followed, quiet, composed, anticipating. Jace rose to his feet.

"When will you propose?" Bella asked, impertinent but adorable.

Jace playfully pressed a finger to his lips for Bella to be quiet before looking at Millie. "I shall be back in the morning."

"With a ring, I hope," Bella quipped.

They all laughed and Millie took Jace's arm to lead him out.

Sarah went upstairs to her room to have a bath. It

had been a long day, but she quite liked how it had ended.

It was Millie's first season and she had already secured a suitor who would likely become her husband. It would be several years before Bella would be presented to society, and that gave Sarah enough time to turn her into a proper lady.

With Mrs. Fowler's help, Sarah had a warm bath and she was brushing her light brown hair at the vanity table when a soft knock sounded on her door.

"Come in," she called.

Millie entered. "Do you have a moment, Sarah?" she asked.

"Of course." She put down her hairbrush and moved to her bed, patting the spot beside her for her sister to sit. "So, what is on your mind?"

"Thank you for giving us your blessing."

"You know I want what is best for you. Do you truly love him, Millie? I don't want you to accept his offer unless you do."

Her sister smiled. "I do love him. Very much."

Sarah gave her hand a little squeeze. "Then all is well."

Millie still worried her bottom lip as she looked nervously at Sarah.

"What is it?"

"I want to tell him about the debt. I know that he is aware of the circumstances of Father's death and that we owe some money, but he should know the extent before he commits to marrying me."

A long sigh pushed its way out of Sarah. "All right. Tell him when you get the chance. But be sure to let him know that he will not be taking up any responsibility besides you as his wife."

"I will." She appeared to be more at ease now. "Who visited you at the shop earlier?" Apparently, Millie had not forgotten.

"The Raven," Sarah replied with another sigh.

Millie blanched. "Did he come for his money?"

"He came with an offer. If I help him track down someone, he will forgive the debt," she replied solemnly.

"Who does he want you to find? And shouldn't the police or a private detective do that for him?"

"It's unclear to me why he wants me to do it. You remember that man who kidnapped Libby? The one who was murdered?" At Millie's nod, she continued, "His real wife, the woman who killed him, has a necklace. Apparently it belongs to the Raven and he wants me to find her and help him get it back."

"Are you going to do it?"

She shook her head. "I don't know. I don't want to."

"But we would be free if you did this."

"I know, Millie. It's very tempting but I don't want to put any of you in danger. Look what happened to Detective DeHavillend, and Libby." Detective DeHavillend had been wounded by a man Mrs. Hart had hired to follow him and her dear friend, Libby. "She could come after you or Bella if she knows I'm looking for her. I can't risk that."

"What if we stayed with Jace while you're searching?

His house in Beacon Hill is large and well-staffed. I doubt anyone could hurt us there."

She had a point, of course, but Sarah didn't want them burdening Jace like that. He was not even married to Millie yet.

"It wouldn't be right. It's best if I just continue to work hard to pay it off. This offer is an easy way out and quite often things that look easy, are not. It could backfire."

Millie's shoulders slumped a little. "I should think it's a risk worth taking. Father has been most unfair to us and it will be tragic if we spent the rest of our lives paying for something *he* did."

Sarah closed her eyes and tried to ignore the opposing voices in her head. On the one hand, it would be liberating to have the debt removed from her shoulders. On the other, the possibility of danger was real.

"I'll have to think more about this," she said after a short moment.

"I trust you, Sarah," Millie said. "I trust you will decide what is best for this family."

It was so much responsibility. Even though she had sisters who supported her, Sarah still felt quite alone sometimes.

CHAPTER THREE

The following evening

As promised, Jace arrived at Sarah's house at seven to accompany them to Lady Dianne's engagement ball. When Sarah had returned home from the shop an hour earlier, she had been tempted to spend a quiet evening at home, but knowing how much Millie wanted to attend the ball, she had forced herself to get dressed.

If Millie was going with Jace, someone had to play chaperone and there was no one but her.

They were now officially engaged. Jace had arrived that morning with a beautiful diamond ring, a family heirloom, and certainly the most expensive piece of jewelry to ever circle Millie's finger. Bella still sighed dreamily whenever she saw the ring.

"I fear I won't be able to keep my hands down

tonight," Millie said as they walked downstairs to meet Jace.

"Most newly engaged ladies can't." Sarah chuckled.

Millie was wearing a pale blue dress that matched her eyes beautifully. Her tiny waist was cinched so tight by her corset that Sarah wondered if she could truly breathe. She had never liked corsets and only wore them because they were in fashion and her figure looked better in them. Unlike Millie, whose figure could be termed ideal, Sarah was far less shapely and very tall.

Jace's eyes roved Millie longingly when they entered the drawing room and he almost forgot to bow in greeting. Sarah smiled. She had carefully made all of her sister's dresses for her first season. They were the latest fashion and she always looked beautiful but tonight, Sarah had put in even more effort in dressing Millie. And she was proud of the result.

The journey from their home to Belleville House in Jace's carriage took longer than expected. Every Boston elite was in attendance and this ball would no doubt be called the event of the year.

It took them more than half an hour to make it the last few blocks to the entrance, due to the line of carriages. They were relieved when they were finally inside the house.

Jace swept Millie away to begin introducing her as his fiancée, while Sarah was left to find her way around the opulent ballroom. She was used to attending these events. As a matter of fact, she attended at least one a week, yet she often felt out of place. Especially today. She was not here as a member of the elite. Not anymore. She was here because people valued her skill as a designer and seamstress.

The ballroom was bright and colorful with ladies dressed and bejeweled in all sorts of creations. Sarah usually studied their dresses—even the ones she had made—for new ideas and oftentimes, she found the inspiration she was looking for. But she didn't feel like doing that, tonight.

There was something in the air that made her uneasy and she couldn't define it. A feeling of foreboding. An awareness of something—or *someone*—out of the ordinary.

She was heading toward the refreshment table when a hand at her elbow stopped her progress. When she turned, she found Libby beaming at her. Her friend looked positively radiant. Did all newly engaged women look like that?

No sooner had that question popped up in her thoughts than Duchess Trevallyn joined them, and she looked just as radiant as the baroness.

Both women pulled her into a hug one after the other before asking how she was. She was not all right, but she couldn't tell them that so she pasted a smile on her face and said, "I'm fine."

"Are you sure?" Libby asked. "You look a bit uneasy."

She laughed to mask the truth. She *was* feeling uneasy. "Millie is here somewhere, of course. I'm just a little nervous."

Anna Trevallyn laughed. "She's engaged now. You shouldn't be worrying as much as you did before."

"I think I should be worrying more now," she mumbled, then realized something. "How did you know?"

"We couldn't miss it with the way Mr. Campbell is showing her off," Libby said.

"With the attention she's getting, Millie might just be the belle of the ball." Anna adjusted her satin gloves and grinned.

"That wouldn't be fair on Lady Dianne," Sarah said, looking around the ballroom for the lady in question. She spotted her in the middle of a small crowd of giggling girls. Sarah's height was rather advantageous in ballrooms, for it allowed her to spot people more quickly. Next, she looked for Millie and found her in the middle of a crowd, too.

"So, how is the dress we've been hearing so much about coming along?" Libby asked, drawing Sarah's gaze back to her friends.

"I have finished working on it. The final fitting took place this morning."

"Is it all it is being reported to be?" Anna asked. "Though I'm sure it is, given your expertise."

Sarah shrugged. "I made what Lady Dianne wanted and added a little more." She felt a measure of satisfaction in saying that. Lady Dianne had drawn attention to her dress by announcing that it would be one of the most beautiful wedding dresses ever made, piquing the curiosity of most.

"Oh, Lady Sarah!" someone called from behind her.

She turned her head slowly in the direction of the voice to see Miss Rosemary Sherriden.

"What's Lady Dianne's dress like?" Miss Sherriden asked. Sarah had the feeling she might be hearing that question all evening.

She smiled, without forcing it this time, and said nothing.

"Oh, you!" Miss Sherriden laughed. "Why must you be tight-lipped about this?"

Libby rolled her eyes. "Honestly, Miss Sherriden, have you ever seen a lady reveal her wedding dress before the actual day?"

Before Miss Sherriden could respond to that, another lady joined them. Sarah recognized her face, but for the life of her, she could not remember her name.

"Lady Sarah, Lady Dianne has been praising your skills all evening. I would like you to make my wedding dress, please. Can you call upon my house tomorrow so we may talk more about it?"

"Yes, of course," Sarah replied, making a mental note to ask Libby or Anna the woman's name.

"I think I want you to make my dress too, Lady Sarah," Miss Sherriden put in.

"And mine," Anna said lightly.

Sarah's brow rose inquiringly.

"I am serious." Anna was smirking, but her sharp blue eyes told Sarah just how serious she was.

A sense of pride filled her at that moment.

Perhaps this was how the Raven felt about his accomplishments. She had built her dress design business from nothing, and now, she was being sought after by everyone. It was, indeed, a very gratifying thing. Although Sarah would not allow pride to take command of her, she could appreciate what she'd built because she had worked hard for it. If the Raven had this sense of pride in his businesses, it could surely explain some of his arrogance.

As if her thoughts had conjured him up out of thin air, the Raven appeared at the ballroom entrance. Instantly, the atmosphere changed and all chattering ceased. Naught was heard but the strains of a waltz continuing from the orchestra. He stood there tall and proud, regarding the gaping crowd with a mixture of boredom and condescension. His gaze caught Sarah's and he tilted his head slightly.

Then he strode forward and the crowd parted for him. His incredibly green eyes never left Sarah as he advanced toward her. Knots began to form in her stomach and the closer he got, the tighter they became.

Once he reached her, the Raven bowed in a courtly manner and murmured, "Lady Sarah," before holding out his hand for her to take.

THERE WAS ONLY ONE REASON TAM HAD DECIDED TO attend this event, and that was to see Sarah. To speak with her, to be exact.

One would argue that visiting her shop or her home was more logical, but Tam admitted to himself that his logic was questionable whenever it came to this woman.

He didn't have to look through the crowd too hard to find her. Apart from her uncommon height, she was wearing the most eye-catching red satin dress. Among this simpering pastel-and-frills crowd, she stood out like a rare jewel. Something kicked in his chest.

Her gray eyes were electrifying as she studied him. And that dress...

No, it was not the dress, he decided. It was *her*. Sarah was not the sort of woman one would call pretty by society standards but by God, she did things to his pulse rate. She had a unique sort of beauty that many failed to notice, and it pulled him in like nothing else.

Everything in his periphery blurred. His vision was focused only on her.

"Lady Sarah," he murmured, extending his hand as he bowed. "Will you dance with me?"

She blinked in surprise but regained her composure rather quickly. To his relief, Sarah did not leave him dangling. Instead, she placed her hand in his and allowed him to lead her to the dance floor. His arm encircled her waist and he pulled her as close as decorum would allow.

"What are you doing here?" she asked through clenched teeth.

He smiled. "I was invited, just like you."

"I know you were invited but you hardly ever grace these events with your presence."

They began to move around the dance area. She was such a graceful dancer.

"Have you made a decision?"

Her eyes snapped up to his, hard as steel. "You gave me three days."

"I don’t believe you have that luxury anymore."

“I beg your pardon? Why not?” Her eyes blazed. How she must dislike him.

"I need that necklace back as soon as possible. Before she leaves the country altogether."

"She might leave?"

"She is wanted by the police. She will do anything to avoid being caught and that includes exiling herself."

They were conversing barely above a whisper. The closeness of their bodies defied propriety and many eyes were fixed on them. He should care, for her sake, but she was in his arms once more and he was damned if he would let her go.

"Very well,” she announced.”

“You will do it?”

“I will do it, but have a condition," she said.

He twirled her twice before answering.

"What is your condition?"

Sarah's light brown hair shone almost golden under the chandelier above them and a stray lock had fallen gently over her bare shoulder. He could reach out and stroke it, but he restrained himself. Not because of their audience but because he knew she would hate it.

"I need assurance that no harm will come to my sisters. They will be at home by themselves with an aging housekeeper and butler. I need to know you will do something to keep them safe."

He inclined his head and regarded her as they moved. She was right to be concerned for her sisters. Anyone with their best interests at heart would be.

"Do you trust that I keep my word?"

She frowned. "I might not like you, Tamworth Arbusson, but I do know you always keep your word, when you give it."

"Good. Then trust me when I say I will protect your sisters. They can come and stay in Raven Hall until you've finished your mission."

"Raven Hall?" She sounded surprised.

"Yes. A large manor house on a property right at the north edge of Boston, overlooking the sea. It is very picturesque. They will be safe there."

Sarah gave him a dubious look.

"Since you appear to require more assurance, I'll have you know that Raven Hall is my home."

"Ah."

"It is well-guarded. In fact, it is probably one of the safest locations in Boston, for your sisters to remain cared for at the present time. I myself, can stay at my club, if you don't wish me to be there, but I do assure you my staff are well-trained, and they will look after your sisters impeccably until your return."

She was quiet for a while and he thought she was going to refuse, until she suddenly announced, "All right."

"Good. I'll send a carriage for them tomorrow

morning. You can accompany them to see the place if that will give you some peace of mind."

"I will do that." She cleared her throat. "Thank you," she said gruffly. It was clear she did not want to be indebted to him any more than she already was, but she was a smart woman, and she had quickly seen that this was a sensible offer.

He quirked a smile, appreciating her determination to protect her sisters. She reminded him of himself sometimes. If he'd had anyone to protect, he would do everything in his power to ensure their wellbeing…

The thought hit him out of nowhere. He *did* have someone to protect…

The waltz came to an end and he tucked her hand into the crook of his arm and steered her away from the dance floor. Eyes were still on them as they made for the ballroom exit.

"What are you doing?" Sarah asked, a look of consternation casting a shadow over her face.

"Taking you out of the ballroom," he supplied as they neared the door.

"Why would you do that? Have you no care for my reputation?"

He chuckled. "Your reputation was tarnished the moment I danced with you." When her eyes bulged out, he said, "I jest."

"Well, that was not funny." They were out of the ballroom now and he was walking her toward a salon at the end of the hall.

"I think it is. I also think worrying about your

reputation is a waste of time. It is not as though you intend to marry."

She turned to glare at him but he looked straight ahead, pretending not to notice.

"What do you mean by that?" she questioned.

He did not reply until they were ensconced in the salon. He waved for her to sit on one of the red damask sofas as he moved to a side table laden with decanters and empty snifters.

"Are you very familiar with Lady Dianne?" Sarah asked as she lowered herself onto the sofa, a dubious look in her eyes.

"No, I am not." He poured some whiskey into two snifters and offered her one, before sitting in a chair opposite and languidly stretching his long legs before him, crossed at the ankles.

"You seem to know your way around quite well."

He shrugged. "Her brother, Rupert Belleville, is an acquaintance."

One skeptical brow rose as she cast him a glance before taking a sip of her drink. "I wouldn't feel that comfortable in the home of a mere acquaintance," she observed.

Most people with the same relationship he had with Rupert Belleville would consider him a friend, but Tam did not allow himself to become close to people that way. Having friends meant showing his vulnerabilities and he did not operate in that manner. Only two people had seen his vulnerable side and he much preferred to keep that number stable.

"That is because you care too much about people's opinion of you. Which brings us back to the topic of your reputation. You have no intention of marrying, so why bother about what people think?"

"Quite the inference," she murmured, seeming to relax a bit.

Taking her away from the ballroom appeared to be doing her some good. But he doubted she was aware of that.

"And you couldn't be more wrong," she added.

"Is that what you tell yourself? Do you truly believe you have eliminated marriage from your plans?"

Her expression darkened. "What makes you think you know me so well?"

"You're not an easy woman to read, but I have my ways. I know you better than you think."

She rolled her eyes and raised her glass to her lips, momentarily drawing his attention to them. Something like regret stirred within him. Every moment he spent with Sarah reminded him of what he had let fall from his grasp, and the probability of never regaining it.

"Well, it's been a nice chat." She set her half-drunk liquor down on the small table beside her and rose, smoothing away any wrinkles that had formed on her dress with slim, deft hands.

"Just where are you going? We have not finished talking. We have hardly begun, in fact."

"You are talking nonsense and I do not wish to be a part of it."

"I brought you here to discuss business." That was a

lie. There was no business to discuss now that they hadn't already discussed. He just wanted to keep her with him a moment longer.

Sarah sat back down. "What is it?" Her gaze turned nervous.

"This job I have given you comes before your dressmaking work," he said, at first for the lack of anything better to say, but then he realized the validity of his request.

"You cannot seriously suggest that." Her voice rose a notch. "The demand for my work is increasing."

"Yes," he drawled, "I am well aware of your rising popularity. This is as important to me as I am sure settling your father's debt is to you. I need you to take it very seriously."

"I do take this very seriously, Raven…"

He gritted his teeth at her use of his moniker. She knew his name like she knew her own. She had spoken it with passion in her tone when they had been together in the past. And now she called him Raven like everyone else. Did he truly mean absolutely nothing to her anymore, as she claimed?

"…but you cannot seriously expect me to abandon my customers to roam the streets of Boston in search of a thief." She sighed. "I will give this as much priority as I can, but I will also attend to my own business. You are not the only person to whom my father owed money."

It was rather unfortunate that she had all these debts to pay. He had learned that when her father's title had passed to her cousin, the latter had shirked both the responsibility to pay the debts, and the responsibility of taking on care of the Smith-Jones family. Instead, it had all fallen to Sarah.

"As long as you will make my task a priority, I don't think we will have a problem," he drawled.

"Is that all you wanted to discuss?"

He nodded and she rose. "Have a good night," she said, as she crossed the room to the door. She was clearly upset. It was apparent in her tone as well as her posture.

Giving himself no chance to caution against what he was about to do, he bolted to his feet, crossed the room, and took hold of her arm before she could exit.

"You are upset," he said.

"How very observant of you," she said with some irony.

"I don't want you upset with me."

"Why do you care what I feel? People's feelings mean nothing to you."

"Do you honestly think that?"

"Yes. You would have been kinder to us if you truly cared."

Her words raised Tamworth's ire. "I have never demanded what is owed to me and you know that. I have let you be for two years, and when I decided to show myself, it was with an offer to make it easier for you to settle the debt. What more do you want me to do?"

She looked away without responding. He understood what she wished for, and yet, he couldn't grant that wish. It would set an unhealthy precedent. That was why he had come with this admittedly hare-brained offer. He wanted the ability to let her out of her obligation in a respectable way. He could easily sit at his desk and write up a document to state that he had forgiven the debt but he would not do it. This was better for everyone.

"We can't always have everything we want, Sarah," he said softly, finally reaching to stroke that lock of hair that had teased him all evening. "Life is not fair."

"But you could be." She turned pleading eyes his way.

Very gently, he tucked a long finger under her chin and tilted her face up to his, then lowered his head until his lips were a hairsbreadth from hers. But Sarah turned away, rejecting his kiss.

"I am not that fool anymore, Raven."

With that, she pulled her arm from his grasp and left the room, leaving him standing there on his own like a fool.

CHAPTER FOUR

The following day

Every encounter with the Raven was an opportunity to assert herself as a woman that should not be trifled with, but all Sarah ever managed to do was add more heaviness to the pile of regret weighing down her heart. She had all but begged him to forgive her debt last night. Something she had never done. And something she was deeply embarrassed about this morning.

An hour ago, she had been torn between sending her sisters to Jace Campbell's home to keep them safe and taking the Raven up on his offer of Raven Hall. After careful thought, she had decided to take them to Raven Hall. As much as she disliked being beholden to the man, she knew the Raven would keep his word and ensure her sisters were kept safe. And it was not Jace Campbell's battle, after all. Involving him was not ideal.

Bella's shrill voice rang across the hall to assault Sarah's ears. "I can't find my music box!"

"Leave it! We are running late," Sarah called from the foot of the stairs.

"I can't. It's my favorite thing in the world!" She appeared on top of the stairs, face red and eyes glinting with unshed tears. "You!" She pointed a small finger at Millie. "You took it!"

On Sarah's left, Millie snickered. "Now, what would I gain from hiding your music box? Will you come down here? We're running late and Sarah has to go to work."

"Give me my music box, Millie." Bella's chin quivered as she spoke.

With a long sigh, Sarah climbed the stairs to where her sister stood and took her hand. "Let's go find it."

They entered Bella's room and began to search. Sarah knew her sister would not budge without that music box. It had been given to her by their mother.

"Did you check under the bed?" Sarah asked.

"It can't be there. It's always on my table." She pointed at the small table by the window where she sat and drew pictures. "I told you, Millie took it."

"Here's your music box," Millie said from the doorway. In her hand was the gilded item.

"I knew it!" Bella stomped her feet on the floor then charged toward Millie at full speed. Before she could reach her, Sarah grabbed the green satin sash of the girl's dress to stay her. "Let go of me!"

Sarah held her free hand forward toward Millie. "Give me the box." When she did, Sarah pulled a struggling Bella back and handed her the box. That seemed to placate her and she stopped struggling to get to Millie.

"I hope you are happy with yourself, Millie," Sarah reprimanded.

Looking guilty for the first time since the drama began, Millie looked down toward her feet and mumbled, "I'm sorry."

"Let's go." Sarah brushed past to go downstairs. It was exhausting business running a family.

The Raven had sent a carriage as promised. A well-sprung luxurious black carriage, pulled by a team of fine black horses.

"That's very grand," Bella gasped.

The Smith-Jones' girls didn't have a carriage…not anymore, and although they had ridden in grand carriages many times in the past, none had been as grand as this. Bella was right to be awed.

A footman opened the door and Bella rushed forward. Sarah could caution her, ask her to comport herself, but she didn't. There was too much going on for her to nitpick regarding manners, or lack thereof. Sarah climbed in after Bella and Millie, and settled in the front-facing seat next to Bella. The ride to Raven Hall would take a while and this was sure to be an eventful ride.

"How long before we reach his place?" Bella asked.

"If it doesn't rain, we should be there in about one hour," Sarah replied, peering out the window at the graying sky. "It looks like rain, though."

The twelve-year-old huffed out a breath. When Millie brought out a book, Bella straightened in her seat and craned her neck. "What are you reading?"

"A book," Millie replied without looking up.

"I know it is a book, Millie. I am not blind. *Which* book?"

Millie sighed. "*Titus Andronicus*."

Bella wrinkled her nose. "Why would you be reading that?"

"Why should I not? Now, be quiet. I need to concentrate."

Bella turned to Sarah. "What will you do to pass the time?"

"I also brought a book," she replied, pulling a tome from her purse: William Dean Howells' *A Hazard of New Fortunes*.

"And neither of you told me so I could bring a book myself?"

Sarah pulled out another book, *A Christmas Carol*, and handed it to her sister. "Don't worry. You won't be miserably bored on this journey."

Bella scrunched her nose. "I don't want that book. It's for little children. And don't tell me you brought that because Christmas is coming. It is not even Thanksgiving yet."

Sarah bit back a sigh, and with great patience, pulled out yet another book. "Will this one do, then?"

Bella wrapped her fingers around the leather-bound volume and traced the gilt title: *The King of the Golden River*. "I think so," she replied as she opened the book.

"Well, I don't have any more," Sarah informed her.

She opened her own book and tried to focus. Reading had now become a luxury, for she hardly had the time anymore. All she usually wanted to do after coming home from her shop was to have a bath, eat dinner with her sisters, and go to bed. If there was an invitation to a social event, she would dress and attend out of duty rather than pleasure. Sarah had once enjoyed these events, but now they always left her feeling drained. She attended only to maintain her connections and gain patronage for her business.

As her eyes moved over the words on the page, her mind wandered to Tamworth Arbusson. Contrary to what she called him to his face, in her mind, he was still Tamworth. She called him Raven on purpose, to needle him. His eyes darkening and his handsome features hardening a touch did not escape her attention every time she called him that vile name. But it was for the best. She and her sisters were safer if he believed she didn't care.

The fact that she still had feelings for him was both pathetic and sad. She was alone in her folly, for Tam would never return the sentiment. Not only because he chose not to, but because she now realized he was truly incapable of feeling anything for anyone besides himself.

"How long will we stay with this Mr. Raven?" Bella's voice broke through the prison of her thoughts, freeing her.

"God bless you, child." Sarah released a breath.

Bella beamed. "Truly?"

Sarah smiled at her and tucked a lock of her sister's curly blond hair behind her ears. Something she remembered her mother doing as a gesture of affection. "Truly," she said, and Arabella's blue eyes danced.

"Now, how long will we be staying?"

"I am not sure, but it should not be longer than a fortnight."

"A fortnight is too long."

"I know, my dear," Sarah said softly.

"Why didn't we just go to Jace Campbell's house?"

At this, Millie glanced up from her book and answered Bella's question. "It is not that simple. This is our problem and we should not bother Jace with it."

Bella frowned as though she was in disagreement with her sister. "We hardly know Mr. Raven but Jace we are familiar with. Are you afraid he will decide not to marry you if he finds out that we have a monumental debt to pay off?"

Millie hesitated.

"Oh!" Bella nodded thoughtfully before turning back to Sarah. "And what is Mr. Raven like?"

The chuckle that escaped Sarah's mouth did not contain an ounce of mirth. "He is a very quiet man who may have forgotten how to smile."

Bella sat back in her chair and sighed. "This is going to be a long stay."

Unfortunately, it will be, Sarah wanted to say, but decided that would be unwise.

"Tell me he can tolerate someone like me," Bella said after a moment.

Sarah was certain he wouldn't tolerate Bella. The best thing for her sister to do was to stay out of his way. "He doesn't remain in the house very much. He is usually at one of his clubs."

"So, there is a chance we are not going to see him this morning."

"Yes."

"I would like to meet him, though. It sounds as though he is a curmudgeonly old man with no love in his life at all. Poor old thing."

Sarah didn't bother to correct her. The assessment was not completely off the mark because, in two or three decades, Tam might just be that curmudgeon. He already was a cold cynic with no regard for human emotions…and he definitely had no love in his heart. He had long rejected such a thing.

"I suppose he does not even let sunlight into his rooms."

Sarah laughed at her sister's musings. She had been in *The Barbican* a few times and Tam's office was dark during all of her visits. Heavy velvet drapes had blocked out the light and although some rays had defied the obstruction and shone into the room, the streaks of light only added to the mystery and gloom of his world. She often wondered about how he lived the way he did. She simply could not fathom living like that. It was such a sad existence; to have no love; to have all the money in the world and still want more; to deny others mercy because he had not been shown any in the past.

"I suppose I had best read this book," Bella said, opening the book again.

Sarah did the same. No sooner had she regained her focus and begun reading than Bella's voice came rolling in like a ball.

"How much longer?"

"I don't know, Bella. Just read your book and stop thinking about the time."

"What if it rains?" Her sister looked out the window as she spoke.

"Can you please be quiet?" Millie moaned.

Bella gave an exaggerated sigh and reopened her book.

Two hours later

SARAH WAS THE FIRST TO ALIGHT FROM THE CARRIAGE and the towering edifice before her rendered her legs immobile. She gaped shamelessly. To call this a manor would be a crime, yet Tam had called it that. Oh, she did not think his calling it a manor had stemmed from humility in any way. Perhaps this was a mere manor to one such as him.

The collective gasps from her sisters on seeing the grand structure they had arrived at, confirmed she was not alone in her awe.

"*This* is a manor?" Millie asked.

Although their father had been an earl, his habits

had deprived them of luxuries they ought to have enjoyed. And any little luxury they'd had, had disappeared quickly after his death. Sarah wondered if Millie and Bella had all but forgotten their previous life. Even if they hadn't, they had never experienced anything like the grandeur of Raven Hall.

Disappointment washed over her just then; disappointment at herself and at the way their lives had turned out.

There was no doubt left in her mind. She would carry out Tamworth's quest and somehow free her family from debt. She would do whatever it took… whatever he asked. Within reason, of course.

The structure before them was a little shrouded by the morning fog and although the grounds were obviously well-maintained, autumn had yellowed the grass and stripped the trees and shrubs of their leaves. While it no doubt looked magical in spring and summer, the place appeared haunted now. Beautifully haunted.

"Come, girls," she said, taking Bella's hand in hers and stepping forward.

They walked up a set of marble steps to the black lacquered portal. A chill suddenly ran through her body and before Sarah could lift her hand up to the knocker attached to the mouth of a brass lion, the door swung open. A middle-aged man—the butler, presumably—greeted them. He stepped to the side and waved for them to enter.

Her legs trembled slightly as she crossed the threshold into the entrance foyer. Turning her head, she glanced back at the carriage in the driveway, wondering if it was too late to turn back and go home. When she swiveled again, she found herself fully in the foyer with Bella dragging her forward, toward a man standing at the foot of an enormous sweeping staircase. The Raven.

She stopped and tugged on Bella's hand. Then the Raven stepped forward and gave Bella a smile before bowing to all of them.

"Lady Sarah," he acknowledged, then turned to her sisters. "Lady Millicent, and Lady Arabella, welcome to Raven Hall."

Bella removed her hand from Sarah's and caught up her skirt so she could spread her dress and curtsy gracefully. Before she rose, she looked up and asked, "Is he Mr. Raven's son?"

"I think that is Mr. Raven himself," Millie whispered, her eyes wide.

The Raven's eyes met Sarah's and he quirked a brow in question. She held his gaze and said, "Yes, Bella, that is him."

She had never given the girls his full name and they only knew him as the Raven. To show a bit of courtesy, they had chosen to call him Mr. Raven.

"He is not a curmudgeonly old man," Bella observed, her bright blue eyes fixed on the impossibly tall man before them.

Tam's eyes narrowed and Sarah couldn't help smirking. She was being petty, she knew, but she didn't care. Any chance to be a thorn in his flesh was welcome. He had done far worse to her.

"But the manor *is* very dark," Bella continued, looking around the foyer. "Everything is dark wood and the curtains are not open. Why do you like it this way, Mr. Raven?"

Sarah took that moment to look around her. The walls were paneled with polished dark wood that was identical to the staircase balustrade and rail. Two wooden raven statues stood sentry on post caps on either side of the stairs, their eyes gleaming knowingly…quite like their master's. An archway to her left led into an even darker room while the one on her right showed a drawing room. She stopped counting how many shadowed corners there were. The little light filtering in from between the drapes barely touched anything. If just the foyer could evoke in her a feeling of such dread, she was afraid of what the rest of the manor could do to her…or her sisters.

"It feels warmer like this," he replied, smiling down at Bella.

"You could turn on the lighting. You do have gas lamps in here, do you not?"

"Even better," Tamworth answered. "I have the newest invention. Electric lamps."

He crossed the foyer to flick a switch by an archway. The area was instantly illuminated, the glass chandelier above them coming to life. All three girls gaped upward at the sight. It was beautiful, and Sarah had to admit, definitely not shadowed anymore.

"Better?" he asked Bella.

"Oh, quite so." The young girl turned in a circle,

observing the changes the light had made. "But wouldn't it be just as good to open the windows? Natural light is very pleasing."

Tamworth raised his brows, seeming amused, which quite surprised Sarah. "Really? Tell me more."

"Our house in the city is nowhere near as beautiful as this one, but the drawing room looks lovely every time we open the drapes in the morning."

"Are you sure you're only twelve?" he asked.

"Well, I will be thirteen in ten months."

Tamworth moved to the windows adjacent to the door and pulled the drapes apart to let the morning sunshine through before flicking the switch to turn off the lighting. "What about that?"

Bella held her hands primly in front of her, quite like a schoolmistress, and inclined her head regally. "Much better."

Tam bowed in response.

Sarah was rendered speechless at this point. Not only had he had a conversation with Bella, but he had illuminated his home for her. He met her eyes briefly, and the smile he had been directing toward Bella froze. His eyes hardened momentarily. There was the Raven she knew. He was like two different men.

"Mr. Raven," Millie called.

"Yes, Lady Millicent?"

"May we be shown to our rooms, please?"

"Of course." He walked toward Sarah and held his arm out to her. "Shall we?"

She had no choice but to place her hand on his

forearm and let him lead her up the enormous staircase with her sisters following behind.

"For a man that we owe a lot of money to, you are quite friendly," Millie said from behind.

Tamworth looked at Sarah when he replied. "I am not a monster."

The stairs split on the first landing, heading off to different wings of the manor. A large portrait of a woman graced the wall of the landing. She was a beautiful woman with bright red hair and emerald green eyes that looked very much like Tamworth's. He had told her very little about his childhood, except that he had been raised by his grandmother.

"Who is this?" Millie asked, stopping in front of the portrait.

"She's got such beautiful hair," Bella said dreamily.

Tamworth stopped and turned around, raising his head to gaze at the portrait. His expression was unreadable. "Her name was Regina Ghyslaine Arbusson. She was quite a remarkable woman."

"Was she your mother?" Millie asked.

"Millie…" Sarah warned.

"My grandmother." He turned swiftly and continued up the stairs, pulling her with him. The girls had no choice but to stop staring at the portrait and follow.

They took the staircase on the left, up two flights to the second floor, and walked down a hallway. Like every part of the house she had seen so far, the walls were paneled with the same dark wood. A red floral carpet covered the floor while paintings from well-known artists decorated the walls.

They stopped in front of a door and Tamworth reached forward and opened it before turning to Bella and waving his hand in a gesture for her to enter. "This is your room, Lady Bella," he said.

She walked in, cautiously at first, but quickly brightened when she saw the room. It was decorated in shades of peach, cream, and powder pink. She made for the four-poster bed and sat on it, then looked at them. "I like it." On the other side of the room was a marble fireplace with a small sitting area before it. A door adjacent to the fireplace led into what Sarah guessed would be a dressing room and bathing room.

"I am glad you do." He turned to Millie and said, "Shall we?"

Millie exited the room first. Bella hopped down from the bed and followed them out, curious to see what her sisters' rooms looked like. Tamworth led them to the next door and opened it, waving for Millie to enter. This room was just as pretty as the one assigned to Bella; decorated in shades of mint and olive green, and brown; and set in much the same way with a four-poster bed on one side, a small sitting area by a marble fireplace, plus an escritoire by the window.

The look on Millicent's face confirmed that she liked it, and when they left the room, she did not follow them. Bella, however, dogged their steps like a puppy. The next room was at the end of the hall and while Bella and

Millie's rooms were side by side, this one was on the opposite side of the hall and appeared to be larger.

Tamworth opened the door but before Sarah could enter, Bella was already in and cooing with awe. He released her arm and she walked in. She knew she would have to spend some nights here to be close to her sisters, but she had not expected to be given a room like this.

"You have the best room here," Bella said, trailing her small hands over a midnight-blue damask sofa.

The first room was an entire sitting room, decorated in brown, cream, and midnight-blue, and it connected to the bedroom through an archway made of carved mahogany. Sarah walked through it to the bedroom which was decorated in the same colors as the sitting room.

It immediately became apparent that Tam had chosen this room for her not at random but with great care. While her sisters' rooms had looked cheery and innocent, hers was dark. This room seemed to represent the dark world that she and Tamworth were in. Perhaps he wanted to remind her of it.

"How do you like it?" His voice flowed to her ear from behind.

She turned around to make sure her sister was not within earshot before she said in a low voice, "Why are you doing this?"

"Doing what?" He feigned innocence.

"A queen could live here," Bella's voice rang from

the sitting room. "Why is it dark, Mr. Raven?" she asked, appearing in the doorway.

And just like that, his expression changed from hard and ironic to sweet as he turned to Bella. "I thought Lady Sarah would like it like that."

The girl frowned a little. "She loves bright colors."

"Oh, my mistake then." He turned back to Sarah. "Would you like a different room?"

"Oh, that won't be necessary," she said through clenched teeth.

"Excellent," he drawled. "Let's go have breakfast."

"I really should be heading to work," Sarah interjected. "If I leave now, I'll be in the city by noon. I have a lot to do."

One corner of the Raven's mouth tilted upward. "Surely you can stay for breakfast. We'll leave together afterward."

She sighed. "Fine." She turned to look for Bella but the girl had already disappeared. Sarah had an inkling of where she might be. If her guess was correct, she was already roaming the manor, looking for the dining room.

Tamworth offered her his arm again. Instead of taking it, she brushed past him and exited the room. She stopped at Millie's door and called her for breakfast before going downstairs.

"What's your name?" came Bella's voice.

"Abraham Greene, my lady," a deep voice said slowly. It sounded like the butler.

"Where is the dining room, Mr. Greene?" she asked.

Sarah was starting to think she should not have left

Bella undisciplined for this long. She feared it was too late to shape her. The girl was impertinent, to say the least. Gathering the skirt of her blue and gray taffeta dress, she ran down the stairs.

"Arabella," she called in a stern voice.

The girl turned and smiled sheepishly. "I shouldn't be asking that, should I?"

Well, at least she had the sense to know when she was not acting appropriately.

"No, you should not."

Behind her, Tamworth said, "Please feel at home, my lady. The dining room is this way." He started down a hallway off the foyer.

"Do you know something, Mr. Raven?" Bella asked after they had entered the elegant dining room and she was seated.

"What is it, Lady Bella?"

A footman pulled out a chair for Sarah and she lowered herself onto it. Millie sat on her right while Bella was opposite her on the left side of the head of the table where she supposed Tamworth would be sitting.

"On the carriage ride here, I thought our stay was going to be supremely boring or even downright horrible, but after meeting you, I think it will not be all that bad."

Tamworth smiled at her. "I'm happy you feel at home. But something for you to be aware of. My name is Tamworth Arbusson, not Mr. Raven."

They all gasped.

CHAPTER FIVE

Sarah was a very unpredictable woman, to say the least. She had either told her sisters that his name was Mr. Raven, or they had assumed so and she had not bothered to correct them. Knowing her, the latter was more probable.

He did not know what exactly she had told them about him, but they appeared to have assumed he would be a sad old man with neither a heart nor manners. Tam was not that man. At least, he didn't think he was.

Arabella was looking at her eldest sister when she said, "I didn't know you had another name."

He chuckled. "Very few people know my real name."

She nodded and picked up a slice of toast from the basket on the table and pulled the jam and butter toward her. He leaned toward Sarah and whispered, "How nice of you to give them that name."

"I didn't," she replied in a tight voice.

Her words confirmed his earlier surmise. What was

still beyond his understanding, however, was why she didn't correct them. Had she done it to make him out to be a villain?

But then, if she had, the girls would not be at all comfortable around him, especially Arabella who was fast making herself at home.

"Mr. R—I mean, Mr. Arbusson," Millicent began, "do you live in this house all by yourself?"

"Yes, Lady Millicent. Other than my staff, I am alone here. I don't have any family, if that is what you are asking."

"Are they in another country?"

A large percentage of Boston's residents had arrived from other countries, so her question did not surprise him.

"France," he supplied, and said no more.

"You are French?" She seemed fascinated.

"I am American, but yes, I am of French origin."

"Jace said we could spend our honeymoon in Paris."

He raised his brows, not because he didn't know to whom she was referring, but because he was curious to learn more. Sarah wouldn't tell him anything. He might as well sate his curiosity with her sisters. He glanced in her direction and found her focused on finishing her breakfast.

He smiled inwardly. She truly must be in a hurry. But the carriage taking her back to town couldn't leave without him.

"Oh, forgive me for jumping into telling you about someone you don't know," Millie said. "Jace Campbell is my fiancé." She held up her left hand to show him the diamond ring adorning her finger.

Of course, he knew she was engaged to Jace Campbell, even though the man had only proposed yesterday morning. News traveled fast and most men talked freely in clubs.

"My felicitations," he said, raising his coffee mug in an odd form of salute.

Her face pinkened and she lowered her eyes. She was a very pretty and composed girl. Sarah had done a marvelous job of bringing her up, despite there being just six years between them. Well, Sarah was quite a remarkable woman. Before meeting her, he had only ever thought one other woman remarkable, and that was his grandmother.

"Do you have a set date for the wedding?" he asked.

"We only got engaged yesterday morning, but we are thinking after Christmas."

"Would you not prefer a spring or summer wedding when the flowers are in bloom and there is more sunshine?"

She shook her head. "What's more important to me is the man I'm marrying and not the wedding."

Tam's lips parted slightly. He didn't quite know how to respond to that. Something about her statement moved him more than it should.

"Sarah is going to make Millie's dress," Bella said.

"Of course," he returned, finishing his coffee.

"Are you ready?" Sarah asked him, as he drained his cup.

"Yes."

"Shall we go then?"

Arabella grumbled then.

"What is it, Bella?" Sarah asked.

"Do you have to go?"

Sarah smiled gently at her. "You know I do. You'll be fine here."

She nodded solemnly, her sprightly personality seeming to have become tame. Her sisters were deeply attached to her, it was clear.

“My housekeeper, Mrs. Marsh, will be available shortly to show you both properly around the house, and to keep you company while your sister is out,” Tam said. He hoped that would allay some of the young girl’s sudden timidity.

"Will you be coming back tonight?" Bella asked.

"Of course, I will." Sarah pushed back her chair and rose to her feet.

Tam immediately rose, too. "Feel free to explore the house while we're gone," he said. “With or without Mrs. Marsh.”

"I thought you would be hiding something here," Sarah muttered wryly. It was the first time she had joked since their arrival.

"Do you know me to hide things?" He took her arm and led her out of the dining room.

"I know nigh on nothing about you," she said when they were out of the girls' earshot.

"You never asked." He stopped and turned to face her.

"Would you truly have told me if I had asked?"

"Yes."

She continued walking toward the front door, seemingly disbelieving him. The carriage that had conveyed them from South End was waiting in the curved driveway. He held out his hand to help her in, expecting to be rejected.

But she surprised him by placing her small hand in his. Tam clutched it, wanting to hold on for longer than she should, but as soon as she climbed into the carriage, she pulled her hand away to arrange her heavy skirts about her.

Why women chose to wear such hefty garments was beyond him. They were such beautiful creatures, and they hid behind those voluminous garments. He climbed in and settled opposite her.

"Are you going to keep staring at me or are you going to tell me a bit about Raven Hall?"

Had he been staring? He blinked a little, then hid his discomfort by grinning rakishly. Any other woman would have reddened, but not Sarah. Not anymore. She used to blush every time he gave her that particular grin.

"You've hardened over time," he said quietly.

"I beg your pardon?" Her gray eyes narrowed to slits as her fine brows drew together.

Tam decided to change the subject. He didn't want to go down that road with her just yet. "What do you wish to know about Raven Hall?" he asked.

At first, she looked confused but then she released a breath and asked, "Have you had it for long?"

"About a year and a half. It was falling apart when I found it and most of it had to be rebuilt."

"It's quite impressive."

He smiled slowly. "Do you like it?"

"Why does it matter if I like it?"

He shrugged, for show, because in reality, it did matter to him. "Your opinion wouldn't hurt," he said.

"Well, then. It's too dark, as Bella said."

His shoulder lifted in another shrug. "My world is a dark one. You know that."

"You could let some light in."

He had tried once already, and it had not ended well. Tam had been forced to accept his life as it was. Light and happiness were not for everybody.

"Millicent seems happy. It's a love match, then?" he asked, changing the subject.

"Why wouldn't it be a love match?" A dubious look accompanied her words.

"It is very common to arrange marriages for benefit."

Her strong jaw worked to clench her teeth and her eyes blazed. "You're implying that I arranged for her to marry Jace for what we can gain from him." Her voice was filled with anger.

Tam should not have made that implication but it was too late now. To placate her somewhat, he said, "Jace Campbell is a good man and Millicent is fortunate."

She turned to look out the window at the moving scenery.

"Forgive me," he said softly, reaching for her hand.

She pulled her hand away and scooted nearer to the window and away from his reach.

"Sarah," he said in a soft convincing tone. "I didn't mean for my question to sound the way it did. It was with good intentions, I promise you."

She scoffed at that. "You don't have good intentions, Raven. You never have."

"You have such a low opinion of me."

"You've never given me a reason to have a different one."

"Sarah—"

"You turn up after two years of silence and ask me to carry out a difficult task without so much as giving me a choice."

"I did give you a choice, actually."

"You made me an offer."

"An offer you could have refused."

"You claimed to have given me three days to decide and then demanded I decide the following day."

"Sarah, you had reservations and I made you another offer."

"This is exactly what I am talking about. You assert authority under the guise of good intentions. You control people's lives and fortunes."

Her words pierced through him like a sharpened butcher's knife through game. "Is that why you rejected me?"

Sarah had lowered the screen shielding what lay

behind those eyes and he saw what she was truly feeling inside. Pain.

"I rejected you for a lot of reasons, Tamworth,"—his name sounded bitter coming from her mouth—"and your disregard for people's plight was one of them."

That empty space in his heart started to fill, and not with happiness. If she could think this poorly of him, then perhaps he truly was beyond redemption.

He thought back over their conversation, and after a while said, "Jace Campbell is a lucky man, too."

She nodded stiffly but didn't respond further.

Not saying anything more, he leaned back in his seat, holding in the sigh that threatened to rise up from his chest.

He closed his eyes and let the rest of the journey pass in silence.

Two hours later

THAT WAS THE MOST UNCOMFORTABLE CARRIAGE RIDE Sarah had ever experienced. She could not be more glad that it was over. The tension had been so palpable that one could cut through it with a knife, so to speak.

When the carriage rolled to a stop in front of *La Robe Dorée*, Tamworth alighted and held a hand out to her. For a brief moment, she contemplated rejecting it and jumping down by herself, but then she imagined falling on her face in the mud, and finally she accepted his offer of help.

"I'll return in the evening," he said, holding an umbrella that a footman had earlier passed to him over her head. It was raining lightly and very cold, too.

She gave him a nod and left him to enter her shop. She had sent word to Camilla earlier that morning to handle things until she arrived, but nothing had prepared her for what awaited her when she walked in. There were more than a dozen impatient women in the shop and Camilla was running helter-skelter trying to attend to them all.

Miss Sherriden was the first to see Sarah and she rushed over. "Oh, Lady Sarah, you're here! I want you to start with my dress."

"I believe I asked her first last night so she should start with mine," said the lady whose name still escaped Sarah.

Before Sarah could really grasp what was happening, she was swarmed by all the ladies talking all at once, making demands she was not comprehending. Poor Camilla. This must have been what the girl felt.

She coughed and shouted, "Ladies!"

They fell silent at once.

Sarah cleared her throat again to relieve the strain her shouting had put on her voice. "Ladies, let's be civilized, please. We are, after all, well-bred, are we not? I will take your orders one by one. Please settle down."

They obeyed. It was a good thing that her shop had enough seats to accommodate all of them. She arranged for Camilla to make tea for everyone, and then one after the other, she took their orders. Half of them wanted wedding dresses made and the rest wanted day dresses and ball gowns. She fixed the times and organized their demands efficiently. It took her mind off the man who was occupying her thoughts, even if only for a little while.

Three o'clock

"I BELIEVE I CAN AFFORD SOME TIME TO MYSELF NOW," Sarah muttered to herself as she finished sketching a dress on her drawing pad. It was to be Eleanor Peabody's wedding dress—the woman she had been unable to place earlier. She had finally gotten the woman's name while taking her order. "I will be going out now, Camilla. I will be back before we close."

"Yes, ma'am."

"If another army of ladies come in, please tell them to come back tomorrow." She retrieved her cloak from the rack near the door and covered herself before placing a gray satin bonnet on her head.

Stepping out into the cold street was just the start of her battle, for it took her a while to find a hire carriage to convey her to Beacon Hill. Camilla might have to close the shop without her, but she would return, nevertheless.

The journey to Armstrong-Leeds House was fast, at

least, and once she had arrived, she asked to see Baroness Esk. She had to start her search somewhere and what better person than one of Mr. Hart's victims? Libby Armstrong-Leeds had been kidnapped and held captive by Mr. Hart, and she had spent quite some time investigating the man's death with her now-fiance, Viscount—or rather, Detective, as he preferred to be known—DeHavillend.

"By the look of you, I suspect this is not a regular social call," Libby said when she entered the drawing room.

"I'm afraid it's not," Sarah replied, hugging her friend before they both took a seat on one of the sofas. "I need your help."

"Whatever you need."

Sarah had given Libby that exact response when the latter had come to her for help all those weeks ago. It was comforting to hear the sentiment being returned with equal fervor. Though Sarah suspected that, when Libby heard her request, she might not be quite as amenable.

"I need to locate Mrs. Hart," Sarah said. "And I need to do it quickly."

Libby's eyes widened.

CHAPTER SIX

"Why on earth do you need to find *that* woman?" Libby asked, consternation darkening her expression.

The reaction was not unexpected, given what Mrs. Hart had put Libby through a few short weeks ago.

"The necklace that she escaped with does not actually belong to her. She stole it from someone else and they need it back."

"Oh, dear." Libby looked even more worried. "I'm so sorry, Sarah, I didn't realize it was not hers. I would never have let her get away with that if I'd known."

Sarah gave her friend a small smile that she hoped would set her guilt at ease. "She convinced you that it was hers. Please don't blame yourself, Libby."

"What do you need?" Libby asked, looking determined to help her friend.

"I understand the police are searching for her, and

Detective DeHavillend is privy to any information they might have."

"Yes. I do know something, too. There are reports that a woman matching her description was seen with two men leaving Roxbury. And then the same woman was apparently spotted in Charlestown with some other men. From the information gathered on the streets, the belief is that the woman is definitely Mrs. Hart. My guess is that, since she does not like to move alone, Mrs. Hart hires thugs to be her bodyguards and carry out her dirty work. She probably went to Charlestown to hire, now that everyone is looking for her locally."

"That makes sense. I can start with Charlestown. Maybe I can find something there."

"Precisely." Libby got to her feet. "Let me change out of this dress and we'll go together."

Sarah's eyes widened at that suggestion. "Where do you think you are going?" Her hand shot out to grab Libby.

"I am coming with you, of course. I want that woman found, too."

A sigh was drawn from Sarah as her mind tried to find a way to stop. This was Sarah's task, not Libby's, and she had to complete it alone. If something happened to her friend, on top of everything else Libby had been through recently, she couldn't bear it. "I can't let you come, Libby. That is to say, you are likely still reeling from the events of the past several weeks and it would not be right to drag you into this."

"Oh, please! I am fully recovered. Sarah, I want justice and I want that woman found."

"Your brother is His Royal Highness, Prince Penforth, and your fiancé is the famed Detective DeHavillend. What do you think they will do to me if I drag you along and something else happens to you?"

Libby's brother was a man no one trifled with. His demeanor alone was certain to send chills racing across one's skin. He was a retired naval officer and protective of his family. Beside his mother and sisters, only one woman had ever seen his softer side and that was Lady Anna Trevallyn, to whom he was now engaged to be married.

Detective DeHavillend was a ruthless investigator whose job for years had been to find those who perpetrated crime. Libby had these men protecting her. Sarah was not so foolish as to drag her to Charlestown of all places. Roxbury was bad enough, but Charlestown…

"They will have me drawn and quartered before I know what hit me. I will not allow it."

"Save your arguing, Sarah. I am coming with you." With that, she drifted out of the room and Sarah heard her giving instructions to someone. She craned her neck and leaned forward from the sofa. Libby was talking with her butler. "Don't let her out of your sight."

"Truly, Libby?" Sarah called out. "You want to hold me prisoner?"

"You can't win here, Sarah," Libby threw back. "In

fact, if you head off without me, I will have no choice but to follow you. Much safer if we travel together."

Sarah slumped back into the sofa and released a shaky breath. In actuality, she would not mind having Elizabeth with her. Having a companion might embolden her. It certainly provided some assurance that she was not completely alone. Though her sense of comfort probably derived from the fact that it was Libby accompanying her. If it had been Tamworth, she would have been filled with unease. No one discomfited her quite like the Raven. And no one had ever made her feel more alone in this world than he had.

After a moment, she realized that the longer she sat there, the more thoughts of Tamworth floated into her mind. She stood up and walked to the window, aiming for distraction. The drapes had been pulled aside and the afternoon sun that had forced its way through the dense Fall cloud cover filtered into the room. She held her face up to the light and closed her eyes, wishing the warmth of the sunlight would penetrate into her heart.

Sarah knew her heart had been left cold, barren, and battered for too long. Those in whom she had placed her trust and faith had betrayed her in the worst possible manner. There had been no choice but to shrink into a dark corner to protect herself.

"I am ready," came Libby's voice. "Honestly, I thought you would try to push past Antoine and leave without me."

"I may have been knocked down by life, but I am still a lady and I still have manners," she jested.

"I wish you would stop saying you have been knocked down, Sarah. Just look at you. Look how far you have come, despite everything." Libby was now standing in front of her and she took Sarah's hands in hers. "You are more than a lady. You are Sarah Smith-Jones, one of the toughest and most fiercely independent women I know. You are someone I admire greatly."

Sarah swallowed the lump that formed in her throat. Libby's words touched her and she appreciated their friendship now more than ever.

"Thank you, Libby," she said softly, then quickly sobered. "We should leave now."

The carriage she had hired for the journey was waiting outside as she had instructed. When they boarded and settled in to the cushioned seats, Sarah noticed what her friend was wearing. A plain gray dress with violet trimmings. There was quite a contrast between this and the peach-colored day dress she'd worn earlier. Sarah was not surprised. This woman had been accused of murder and she had crept around the streets of Boston searching for clues until she managed to clear her name. Libby knew how to appear inconspicuous when she needed to.

When she had come to visit Sarah at her shop a few weeks ago, Libby had been disguised as a widow. It turns out that when people see a widow, they tend to avert their gaze. As a matter of fact, Libby had found people avoided her completely, perehaps fearing her grief might be contagious.

"When did you discard the widow costume?" Sarah asked.

"It was too small. I had the dress made more than four years ago and I have grown since then. I had to cinch my corset so tight that breathing properly became an issue. Besides, it was too gloomy."

Sarah laughed a little. "And gray is not?"

"Might I point out that you are wearing gray, too?"

"Hmm. Good point."

"Have you seen today's papers?" Libby asked, adjusting the beaded straps of her black reticule that was looped around her black gloves.

"No, I have not. It has been quite an unusual day, so far."

"There was an illustration of you dancing with the Raven."

Sarah's eyes widened. "Are you serious?"

"Yes. Now everyone is talking about you, your dance with the Raven, and, of course, your exquisite dresses."

"That explains why *La Robe Dorée* was full today," she mused, then looked across at Libby. "What was the detail about the Raven?"

Libby began to list them on her fingers. "You danced too close. The Raven is a rake. He doesn't dance with anyone. You are fortunate. You are unfortunate… Don't mind the gossip sheets, Sarah. It will pass."

She pinched the bridge of her nose and sighed. "I knew something like this would happen. I knew my reputation would suffer."

Libby waved a hand as though to dismiss her

comment as nonsense. "It is not affecting your business. If anything, you are gaining in popularity. I say don't worry about it."

"But my reputation—"

"Is fine." Libby leaned forward, her eyes glinting with curiosity. "What *is* between you and the Raven, if you do not mind me asking?"

Sarah felt her mood darken instantly and she shoved back a stray lock of hair. "It's a long story."

"Would you like to share it?"

If Libby had asked that question prior to today, Sarah would have denied her what she was seeking, but now… Now she felt like she wanted to share some of the story of her misery with someone. It could unburden her, in a way. What was it they said? *A problem shared is a problem halved.*

"You know of the debt my father left, yes?"

Libby nodded, her eyes commiserating.

"The debt is much bigger than what I have told anyone. The portion you are aware of, is in fact just one debt, out of many. There is a much larger overarching debt. I have almost finished settling the small part. The other portion is more than thrice the first one, and it is owed to the Raven."

Libby's eyes misted. "Oh, Sarah! Why didn't you tell me this?"

Sarah just shook her head. When she had initially told Libby and Anna about the debt, they had offered to help her pay it off, but she had politely declined. She did not want to transfer one debt, for another. They had stressed that there should be no debts whatsoever between them; just almost-sisters helping each other out, but she had still declined.

"You know my stand on it all."

"Sarah, what good are we in your life if we cannot help you when you need it?"

Sarah gave her a rueful smile. "You are helping me now, are you not?"

Libby rolled her eyes. "After I forced you."

Sarah shrugged. "I didn't know my family owed Ta—I mean, the Raven—until two years after Father's death. The Raven told me about it then."

"Did he ask for his money right then and there?"

She shook her head. "He knew I could not pay him. He came back two days ago with an offer."

Libby's eyes instantly bulged almost out of their sockets. "No wonder he danced with you yesterday! Did you accept his proposal?"

Any other time, Libby misconstruing her words would have been funny. "No, Libby, it was not a proposal. Why would he make that sort of offer to offset my father's debt?"

Her friend shrugged. "I don't know. He did seem taken with you last night."

"I don—"

"You didn't see yourself, Sarah. It was a *scene.*"

"Fine. He made a different kind of offer. He requested that I help find something that belongs to him, and if I do, he will write off the debt in full."

"That is a very generous offer," Libby remarked,

looking somewhat impressed. She had always been an adventurous soul and any story that carried intrigue was sure to gain her full attention.

"Don't draw that conclusion just yet. He wants me to find the ruby necklace."

"Oh. I see."

"The ruby necklace belonged to his grandmother, Regina Arbusson. It was stolen from his family, and now Mrs. Hart has it."

That pulled a gasp from Libby. "Why does he want *you* to find it, when I am sure he is perfectly capable of locating it himself?"

"Exactly," Sarah said. "I thought that, too. His motive for asking me this favor still does not make sense as to why he wants me to look for it. He runs a network with close links to the less salubrious side of Boston. He surely has access to more information than any of us can imagine, and yet…"

"There is more to this, Sarah."

Now that Libby had voiced the same concerns, Sarah was even more worried than she had been. "Do you think he is being dishonest with me about his real intentions?"

"Yes. Why would he ask you to do something he could do himself? My theory is this: He wants to forgive the debt but needs you to work a little for it so it does not look like he is being soft. Or, perhaps there is something more sinister going on? Though I doubt that, because he might be unusual but he does not strike me as the sort of man to do anything too nefarious."

"Hardly anything about the Raven surprises me, Libby." Sarah leaned back in her seat, thinking about what her friend had just said. Could he truly be attempting to forgive the debt by giving her this task, so that he might save face with others? He was a very unusual man and seemed to have a hidden motive in all of his dealings.

When he had first approached her, shortly after her father's death, she had thought he meant well and had her family's best interests at heart. She had made the mistake of trusting him.

"Libby," she said, straightening in her seat. "We are on our way to Charlestown. A place we know is not very safe for ladies like us. Why would he make me go on a dangerous quest just because he wants to forgive a debt? Would it not have been easier to make me do something else? Perhaps have me make a very complex dress for one of his mistresses?"

"You have a point," Libby agreed. "None of it really makes a lot of sense." She frowned. "The more I think about it, the more confused I get."

Sarah smiled sardonically. "Now you see why people get nervous around him."

"Quite so. The man is a mystery. Do the girls know about this offer? I know you tell them almost everything."

"Yes, they do. I was concerned about their safety and he offered to have them stay at his manor north of Boston. Raven Hall."

"Do you trust him?" Libby asked, her brows furrowed with concern.

"In that regard, yes, I do. I know my sisters will be safe with him."

"All right."

Sarah glanced out the carriage window. She was anxious to reach their destination and see what she could find. Her intention had just been to see Libby and gather some initial information, but once she learned that Mrs. Hart had been in Charlestown, the opportunity seemed too good to pass up. Camilla would have to close the shop without her, today.

"You cared deeply for him, did you not?" Libby asked softly.

Sarah's head turned sharply and she was suddenly lost as to how to respond to that question. Libby and Anna knew about her previous history with the Raven, but Sarah had never disclosed what went wrong between the two of them.

Six months after her father's death, the Raven had called upon her at her aunt Bernice's home, and life as she knew it changed forever.

CHAPTER SEVEN

Four years earlier

"Sarah, there is someone to see you," Aunt Bernice said with a derisive twist of her lips.

Sarah looked up from the sheaf of papers in front of her and, instead of rising and following her aunt out, she asked, "Who is it?"

Aunt Bernice shrugged. "I don't know. He said he knew your father. He is very handsome, though." Her aunt's eyes took on a dreamy look. Bernice had four daughters. One was married and another was of marriageable age. If Sarah knew her aunt well—and she did—the woman was already looking to match her foolish daughter with the stranger in the drawing room.

"Now, come. We can't keep a gentleman waiting."

Sarah put down the papers and followed her aunt out of the room. She disliked receiving visitors now. At first, the visitors had come to offer their condolences.

Then, as the months passed, another type of visitor had begun to arrive—those to whom her father owed money. She had little doubt that this newest guest would be one of the latter.

At the drawing room door, she took a deep steadying breath and kept her expression as non-committal as she could. She had learned not to show vulnerability. Many were out to get her and her sisters now…even the woman whose roof she was currently living under.

The gentleman rose to his feet as they entered. He was very tall and impeccably dressed. Her aunt was correct; this man was incredibly handsome. His green eyes instantly struck her and she stopped in her tracks. They were a vivid shade, quite like emeralds. And if one could discern a person's intelligence from their eyes, she would say he was a very intelligent man indeed. His hair was as black as a raven's feather and as lustrous as silk. She wondered what it would be like to touch that hair; caress it.

Sarah shook her head to recover her senses. What on earth had gotten into her? Why was she thinking of this man in such romantic fashion? He was likely here to quote figures and deadlines for payment at her.

"Lady Sarah?" He spoke in a rich, deep voice.

"Yes," she replied in an even tone. "Good afternoon, sir."

He bent forward and offered her a courtly bow. When he straightened, he introduced himself. "I am Tamworth Arbusson."

"Mister?" she inquired after his title, in order to properly address him.

"Yes. Mister."

Aunt Bernice came forward then. "Mr. Arbusson, allow me to introduce myself. I am Lady Bernice Smith-Jones. Lady Sarah's aunt and her father's sister by marriage. My son, Landon Smith-Jones, is now Earl Waelcombe."

Sarah glanced at her, irritated. The title Landon had inherited had not come with the prestige it ought to, but her aunt did not care. As long as people addressed her son as *Lord*, and the previous incumbent's debt remained with Sarah through a strange quirk in her father's will, Aunt Bernice did not care a whit.

Mr. Arbusson bowed in much the same manner he had earlier. "I am pleased to make your acquaintance."

Her aunt simpered and smiled, even battered her eyelashes at the man. Sarah tried not to roll her eyes. "I will fetch my daughters and introduce them to you."

"That will not be necessary," he said firmly. "I am here to see Lady Sarah."

"Oh." Aunt Bernice was speechless.

"If you would be so kind, I would like a moment alone with her," he requested. His tone of voice was polite, yet commanding. He had an air of authority about him that could not be missed.

"As long as the door remains open for propriety," Sarah added.

"Why, of course." Aunt Bernice glared at Sarah before exiting the room.

She would pay for this later, she knew. Her aunt simply did not like her or her sisters.

She turned to the man in front of her. "Yes?" she inquired, when he did not immediately speak.

"Please sit," he said and again, she was stuck by his commanding presence, his magnetic eyes, and his posture.

It must be a large debt, if he was asking her to sit. She walked over to one of the bright pink sofas in the drawing room and lowered herself onto the edge of it, keeping her back ramrod straight in anticipation of what he might say next.

"Please accept my deepest condolences, Lady Sarah," he said after he had taken a seat opposite.

She inclined her head in a regal manner. "Thank you, Mr. Arbusson."

"How are your sisters?" he asked.

"My sisters are fine," she replied tersely. "But I am sure you did not come here to inquire as to the welfare of my sisters and myself. What can I do for you, Mr. Arbusson?"

One corner of his mouth tilted up in a wry grin, and his eyes glinted as though he found her fascinating. "I came to offer my condolences, my lady, and nothing more."

Sarah was unsure she believed him. "How did you know my father?" she asked.

"He frequented one of my establishments. The Barbican."

She had heard of The Barbican, one of the most

prestigious gentlemen's clubs in Boston. "You own The Barbican?" She was greatly surprised.

"Yes." He smiled at her and her stomach fluttered. If he smiled at her like that one more time, she feared she might start to dream of him tonight.

"You are so young. You cannot be older than twenty-seven."

"Twenty-eight, actually." His tone carried a hint of pride. She did not blame him. If she owned the most prestigious establishment in town, she would want people to know and appreciate her accomplishments.

"The club has been established for three years, but it only started to gain popularity this past year," he explained.

"That…" She released a sigh. Just because her father had gambled everything away, didn't automatically make every gentlemen's club owner a villain. "That is impressive, Mr. Arbusson."

He nodded graciously, accepting her praise. "Were you close to your father?"

Her eyes widened at the suddenness of his question.

"Forgive my impertinence. I should not have asked you something so personal."

Perhaps it was the tone of his voice or the look in his eyes, or even the words themselves, but she felt safe just then; as though he had wrapped his powerful arms around her and promised to keep her safe. Sarah felt heat rising up in her cheeks and quickly covered them with her hands.

If she was to keep from making a fool of herself,

then she would have to refrain from thinking about him in such a romantic manner. Yes, he was attractive, but he was also a stranger. He had an air of mystery that intrigued her, but she needed to be strong and resist. He was only here out of respect, to offer condolences. Nothing more.

With her composure now regained, at least somewhat, she lowered her hands from her cheeks and straightened her back. Having been out in society for two years, she was not unaware of her feminine charm. Sarah was no beauty; as a matter of fact, hardly any gentleman noticed her based on looks alone, but she had learned she had a natural charm that could be employed to excuse certain behaviors—such as being caught blushing.

"Forgive me," she said, fanning her face. "I was a bit overcome just now. To answer your question, yes, we were quite close and he was a good father."

That was entirely false.

CHAPTER EIGHT

Her father had cared about them before their mother's death…or so Sarah vaguely remembered. Sadly, after their mother had given her life to bring Bella into the world, he took a turn for the worse. He was out of the house before they awoke in the morning and they were usually asleep when he returned. Several nights, Sarah would stay up to see him return and when he did, he could barely walk from being too inebriated.

Over time, he got worse. His temper grew short and his patience became almost nonexistent…but only with the servants. When the girls saw him, he tried to hide his state from them, but Sarah knew. The best she was able to do was shield her sisters from what she saw. Whenever they would ask after him, often following days without seeing him, she would tell them that he had been working too hard.

On the night he killed himself, she was mending her

dress in her room. A loud explosive crack echoed through the quiet halls of the house. She dropped the dress and clutched the bedcovers to her chest. That had been a gunshot, and it sounded like it had come from the room opposite hers; her parents' bed chambers. Fear rendered her immobile as a thousand thoughts rushed through her mind, each with a gravity beyond her twenty years.

Footsteps rushing in the hallway snapped her out of her frozen state and she ran out of her room to check what was happening. She saw the butler, Cooper, rushing out of her parents' bed chambers. The housekeeper, Mrs. Fowler, stood crying.

"Go back to your room," Cooper had instructed. Sarah knew then what had happened and she quietly obeyed, but instead of going back to her own room, she went to the room Millie and Bella shared. She sat throughout the rest of the night listening as the house came alive in the most saddening way. It was ironic how peacefully her sisters slept while chaos reigned outside the confines of their room.

When the sun came up, Sarah left the room and crossed the hall. When she reached the door of her parents' chambers, her heart shattered into a million pieces as she faced the truth. A haunting feeling engulfed her. She felt the presence of death keenly at that moment. Death that had not arrived of its own accord, but had been called by a miserable soul. A soul who thought this was the only way out…

She went downstairs, her body so weakened by

shock she had to hold the railing of the stairs to remain upright. She found Cooper and a police constable discussing the situation in the front hall.

"Where is he?" she asked them.

Cooper avoided her eyes. "My lady…"

"My lady," the constable began. "My deepest condolences."

"Where is my father?" She asked again.

"We have taken the body to the mortuary. He will remain there until the investigation is complete. Although the matter is rather conclusive already."

The body. He was no longer her father. He was just a "body" now. In fact, he had ceased being her father a long time ago. Her grief came not from her loss on that night, but from how the loss had come about.

She felt a hand at her elbow and when she turned, she found Mrs. Fowler. The woman wrapped a velvet robe about her and it was then that she realized she had been in her nightdress all this time. "Come, child," she said, pulling Sarah to the kitchen.

Mrs. Fowler made her sit down and poured her some hot tea. "You've had a huge shock. This will help," she said, setting down the steaming mug before her.

"I knew he was in a bad state," Sarah said numbly, "but I never thought he would do something like this."

"Oh, child. None of us ever thought it would come to this." Tears were streaming down Mrs. Fowler's cheeks.

But Sarah's eyes were dry. Her insides were

screaming with pain, but her eyes would not tear up. She forbade them to cry.

He did not deserve her tears.

When her sisters woke an hour later, she went to see them.

"What happened?" Millie asked, the moment she laid eyes on Sarah. They had always been close and could sense when the other was distressed.

"Father is dead," she said without preamble.

To her surprise, Millie did not cry and neither did Bella. They only sat there staring. At first, she thought it was shock, but as the day went by, it became clear that they did not know him well enough to grieve him. Especially Bella, who had never known the sort of man he had been before her birth.

Their cousin Landon and his mother, Aunt Bernice, arrived before noon with Aunt Bernice weeping loudly. Landon at first wore a grim expression on his face, but after the lawyers informed him of his inheritance, he and his mother no longer viewed the situation as a tragedy.

When evening came, Bernice sent her lady's maid to bring some personal items from their house and asked her daughters to come over; all three of them who were still in her care.

And that was how Aunt Bernice made the house her own. At first, Sarah did not mind their presence. She did not mind sharing her home at all, as long as she was left in charge of the affairs of the household as she had always been. Unfortunately, Bernice quickly took over.

Two weeks later

"SARAH," BERNICE SAID AT BREAKFAST. "YOUR COUSIN owns this house now that he has inherited the title. Since your father has not bequeathed it to any of you, the estate has passed on to him."

"I know," Sarah said.

"Good." Bernice smiled falsely. "I just want you to know that, so we can live peacefully together. We will not have any problems as long as you behave yourself."

"Have I done anything besides?" Sarah's voice sounded strange in her own ears. It was devoid of emotion.

"Oh, you haven't, but I am just saying."

Sarah released a breath. "Don't worry, Aunt Bernice. You will have no trouble with us." Her eyes met those of her sisters and they looked as miserable as she felt.

Sarah decided right then to find a new home for her sisters. And to do that, she might have to get married…

But fate had other plans for them. Cooper appeared in the dining room doorway and cleared his throat.

"Lady Sarah," he said. "There is someone to see you. Someone from the bank."

She set down her napkin and slowly rose to her feet. Bernice jumped up, too.

"Why is someone from the bank looking for Sarah?" she asked Cooper.

"He was looking for Earl Waelcombe, and since he is away, he has asked for the former Earl Waelcombe's kin."

"That would be me. I am his sister by marriage." She stepped forward and Sarah allowed it. The woman was eager to assert herself as the new Earl's mother.

They met the man in the drawing room and Bernice did not waste any time, demanding to know what he wanted. Sarah guessed she was after whatever money the man had ostensibly brought with him. But Sarah knew there was no money. Her father had debts unknown to everyone. She had come upon the papers by chance one evening when she had gone looking for him and had found him passed out in his study. Beneath his hand, she had found an undertaking with a large sum owing to someone by her father.

His estate was still being sorted, given how sudden his death had been, but it was only a matter of time before his true material wealth—or lack thereof—was revealed. Landon and Bernice would get the shock of their lives.

"Lady Sarah?" the man asked, looking past Bernice.

Sarah stepped forward and he presented some papers to her.

"I will need a signature on those after you have had the chance to read through them," he said. They all sat, and Sarah read carefully. Her father owed the bank a lot of money and had agreed for the house they were currently living in to be taken as payment in the event that he was unable to pay. His death now meant he was unable to pay and the bank had come for the house.

Sarah and her sisters' lives were about to change drastically, and not for the better. They about to lose the home they had grown up in, not to their cousin and his mother as they had thought, but to the bank.

"My lady, we are deeply sorry," the man said.

No, he was not. Sarah felt numb with horror. She knew the man had been conditioned to convey sympathy regardless of whether or not it was felt. Nevertheless, she did not blame him, for he was merely doing his job. The person to blame for this, was her father.

When she was sure she had read and understood everything in the documents, she rose to her feet with the papers still clutched in her hand and crossed to the escritoire near the window. She retrieved a pen and appended her signature on the paper. She returned to her seat and handed the documents over.

"What is the content of the documents?" Bernice asked.

It appeared the man did not hear her because his attention was on the documents and Sarah did not care to inform her. "We will need the signature of the title holder as well," he announced.

"You can leave it here and I am sure he will sign it when he returns. He is out of town at present."

"Very well," the man responded and rose.

"What is my son going to sign?" Bernice asked frantically. "What is happening?"

Sarah turned to her and said in a dull voice. "The bank is taking the house, Aunt Bernice."

Her aunt slumped in her chair. She must have fainted.

At least she *can* faint, she thought to herself. She looked at the man standing awkwardly and he looked surprised at her lack of action.

"She is shocked by the news," she explained dully. "I will get her some smelling salts." She left the room then. "Do we have any smelling salts, Mrs. Fowler?" she asked when she entered the kitchen.

Mrs. Fowler turned from the sink. "What do you need those for?"

"Aunt Bernice fainted."

"Oh, dear!" The middle-aged woman rushed around opening cabinets and closing them until she found the salts. Instead of giving them to Sarah, she rushed out of the kitchen, asking as she went, "Where is she?"

"In the drawing room," Sarah supplied, following more slowly.

Mrs. Fowler shook the salt crystals onto her palm and held it under Bernice's nose. A moment later, the woman was awake and gasping for air. She held her chest, crying.

"They are taking the house!"

Sarah looked at the poor man standing awkwardly in the room. "You may go," she said.

"Of course," he said and bowed courteously. "I shall return when Earl Waelcombe returns."

"What grief!" Bernice wailed, and Mrs. Fowler lamented with her, trying to comfort the woman.

Her cousins and sisters all rushed into the drawing room then. Millie looked alarmed but Bella seemed more curious. Sarah went to them and drew them aside while the other girls surrounded their grieving mother.

"Father owes money to the bank and they are taking the house," she informed them. She did not see the point in keeping this from them, as it affected them more than anyone else. They were homeless, and they needed to know it.

"Where will we go?" Bella asked in a small voice.

A sharp pain shot through Sarah's heart and she drew her sister into her arms. Then Millie too. "You will have a home. I promise." Her plans changed in that instant. Marriage would not suffice. She would have to look for work. She would do whatever she had to, to provide for her sisters. She had a small amount of money saved, enough to secure lodgings for a few days while she looked for work. She had a good idea of her skill set, and some ideas about where to look. She had to think fast, though, because time was not on their side. The bank would expect them to move out soon, and it was unlikely they could continue to live with their aunt, even if they had wanted to. "Come, let's start packing."

Bella sniffed, causing Sarah to bite the inside of her cheek to keep her composure. "Are we going to leave today?" Bella asked.

"Yes, darling." She pulled away and cradled her sister's face in her hands. "Do you trust me?"

Arabella nodded as rivulets of tears began to stream down her cheeks.

"Then believe that we are going to be all right." She looked at Millie, who was now crying too. "I promise," she said.

"I believe you," Bella muttered, wiping her eyes, then her nose with the back of her hand. Sarah retrieved a clean handkerchief from her pocket as she led them out of the drawing room and cleaned Bella's nose.

"You are a fine lady," she said, trying to smile. "And fine ladies use handkerchiefs, not their hand." That drew a small smile from the little girl.

They went first to Bella's room and began packing her things. They were in Millie's room packing when Bernice walked in. Her eyes were red-rimmed from crying. The woman had truly been moved by the loss of the house, it would seem. Perhaps even more so than the girls who had grown up in the place.

"What are you doing?" she asked Sarah.

"We are packing to leave. We can no longer stay here."

"Good idea. I should go and pack, too." She began to leave the room but paused. "We don't have to leave today, however. We can stay until Landon returns and signs the papers."

Sarah shook her head. "I think is better for my sisters and me to leave as soon as we can."

Bernice sniffed. "I suppose you are right. I cannot imagine how you must be feeling right now. I know I feel like something of mine has been taken from me." She sniffed again. "The girls and I might stay until Landon returns. When you are ready to leave, just let me know and you will be conveyed to our townhouse."

Sarah's eyes widened in surprise. "Townhouse?" she asked.

"Yes. The house we lived in before we moved here. I will send word now for rooms to be arranged for you."

"I thought..." She let her voice trail off. Bernice was offering to let them stay with her.

"Oh, come now, Sarah. You didn't think I was going to have you out on the street all by yourselves, did you?" She looked affronted. "What would society think of me? Besides, Landon is your legal guardian so I am obligated to shelter you. Although now I will have to work doubly hard to see you are married."

Sarah was grateful. Bernice may have had her faults, and although Sarah would not claim any affection toward her, the woman was obviously not without conscience. "Thank you, Aunt Bernice," she said with feeling.

"Yes...well..." She turned to leave. "I will send word now for your rooms to be prepared."

After she had left, Sarah sat down on Millie's bed and heaved a sigh. Her sisters sat on either side of her and Bella rested her head against Sarah's arm. Millie took her hand.

"We are going to be all right," Bella said softly.

"Of course we are," Sarah replied. They had each

other and as long as they remained strong, they would be able to handle whatever came their way.

After they were settled in Bernice's townhouse, Sarah acquired black silk and lace and made herself a dress. They were officially in mourning and thus did not attend social gatherings, but they frequently had callers and Sarah began to subtly introduce society to her skill. The society visitors did not know at the time that Sarah had made all her dresses herself, but her friends Anna and Libby knew, and they complimented her greatly on her ability.

They had her make them ball gowns and paid her. Soon, other ladies became interested in her craft and she began to receive commissions to create dresses.

"You will not turn my house into a tailoring shop," Bernice complained one afternoon when she walked into Sarah's room and saw her fitting one of the ladies who had ordered a ballgown. This was about four months after their loss.

Her cousin Lisa walked in just then, wearing a dress Sarah had made. "She makes beautiful dresses, Mama," Lisa said, twirling in her new blue and cream satin ballgown. "Do you like it?"

"Where did you get that dress?" Bernice asked her daughter.

"Sarah finished it for me just now. It is gorgeous!"

Bernice looked at Sarah then. "Well, I suppose your dressmaking is not so bad. I will allow you to continue if you can keep making fine dresses for Lisa. It is her second season and she needs to draw some attention."

"I will be happy to make dresses for anyone you want, Aunt Bernice."

Her eyes darted to the lady Sarah was fitting. "We will talk about this later," she declared, seemingly checking herself and remembering they had company.

After Sarah's client had left, Bernice returned to the room and closed the door firmly behind her. "Here is what we are going to do. I will allow you to make your dresses and we will share the profit."

"I agree," Sarah replied.

Bernice's eyes widened in surprise. "You do?"

"Yes. You have been generous to us, and it is only fair I return the favor. But Lisa's dresses will not be without pay. Making a dress is a difficult task and I sew some of the dress elements by hand." Sarah had spent her first couple of payments on a treadle sewing machine and saved herself a great deal of time.

"What do you mean not without pay? You just made her a dress—"

"Which she paid me for."

Bernice looked horrified. "You collected money from my daughter? Your own cousin?"

"It is business, ma'am. And as you implied just now, if we work together, there is much to be gained."

Bernice was not happy about that but the prospect of making money through Sarah was obviously greater than her irritation. "Very well, she said. "Make the dresses for Lisa and take your payment from my share."

Sarah smiled. "We have a deal."

Sarah, of course, had other plans. She would give Bernice her share, and deduct the cost of Lisa's dresses from that share, but she was also saving. She was planning on setting up a proper shop and then arranging a house for herself and her sisters.

CHAPTER NINE

After their first meeting, Sarah concluded that Mr. Arbusson was a fine gentleman. He was amiable and kind. She had not, however, expected him to return, at least not so soon after his first visit—only three days.

When Bernice came, again, to her room to fetch her, her aunt gave Sarah awarning. "Listen to me, girl!" She grabbed Sarah's arm. "Lisa is still searching for a husband. I will not have you married before my daughter. Tell that man, whoever he is, to stop visiting. If he intends to court you, you need to let him know you are not ready."

Sarah rolled her eyes and sighed. She was honestly sick of the woman's troublesome and meddling ways. "Aunt Bernice, he is not here to court me. But I will do as you say."

"Good." Bernice straightened her dress and left the room.

Sarah paused near the door for a moment, thinking. She was only agreeing to do what Bernice wanted in order to keep the fragile peace between them. In a few months, she intended to get her sisters out of there and have her own dress shop but she still needed more money. Should Bernice stop her from making dresses, it would be difficult to see her plan through.

Sarah went downstairs to meet Mr. Arbusson and found him seated in the drawing room chatting with Lisa. She almost laughed at Bernice's cunning. She had inserted her daughter in an attempt to catch Mr. Arbusson.

Unfortunately for Lisa, he did not seem like the sort of man to be impressed by a pretty young thing with no brain.

When he saw Sarah, he smiled—that slow curve of his mouth up at one corner—and rose to his feet. "Lady Sarah," he greeted.

"Mr. Arbusson, I did not expect to see you again," she said, "and this soon, at that."

"I don't suppose I could keep away for long."

Today, he seemed different. He had been more serious the previous time. Heat began to creep up her neck into her cheeks and she turned away before he could see. What could she use to distract herself? A tassel hanging out of place on the drapes caught her attention and she crossed the room to set it right.

"Mr. Arbusson, you flatter me," she said.

"And should I not?" he replied. She had her back to him now but she could hear the playfulness in his tone.

Suddenly, she was conscious of her mourning dress. After the first few months, she and her sisters had switched black for demure gray and Bella would not stop complaining. She could hardly wait for the second half of the mourning period to be over so she could return to wearing her beautiful colors.

Sarah was certain she must look older than her age but what could she do? She was supposed to conform to society and observe mourning according to their rules.

She turned and found Lisa glaring at her. Sarah shrugged insouciantly and walked back to the sitting area. She sat in one of the too-soft sofas but made sure she was not sitting too close to Lisa.

"So, what can I do for you, Mr. Arbusson?" she asked him.

"The pleasure of your company." That surprised Sarah. Lisa huffed before storming out of the room.

Mr. Arbusson neither spared her a glance nor did he show her any courtesy by rising to his feet. His eyes were fixed on Sarah.

As much as she wanted him to lavish his attention on her, she had to put a stop to this before it went any further, and things got complicated with Bernice.

"That is a lovely compliment, Mr. Arbusson, but I am afraid I cannot accept such compliments from you."

"Why not?" He watched her carefully.

"I am simply not interested."

He laughed then, as though he could not believe he could ever be rejected by a woman. Well, yes. What woman in her right mind would reject a man this handsome, this intriguing? But Sarah was not in her right mind. She had to survive first and she was now responsible for her sisters.

"You and I both know that is not true," he drawled. There was a gleam of amusement in his eyes.

"And how would you know that? Do you read minds?" she threw back.

"No, Lady Sarah, I do not read minds and neither do I want to. I can read people, however, and I know you are happy to see me. Even if you are not happy living in this house."

"You can't be serious." She turned to look at the drawing room doorway to make sure no one was passing by or within earshot.

Mr. Arbusson laughed again. "And you just proved my point."

"I am perfectly fine," she said tersely.

"You have your guard up now. You feel if you share this with me you might be losing something."

"That's enough. You can stop reading me now." The man was accurate. He must have a deep intuition to understand people this well. Out of curiosity, she asked, "Are you one of those people that studies psychology?"

"Actually, yes, but not in any formal way. My education ended when I was twelve."

"How…I mean, why did your education end at twelve?"

"I was living with my uncle but I left his home at the age of twelve and commenced a life on my own."

Sarah was sure her eyes were bulging out. A twelve-year-old leaving home to live on his own? How utterly terrifying.

"I suppose you are wondering what must have made me leave at such a young age."

"I confess that I am wondering," she said.

"Like you, I was not happy in the house I was living in. I was made to feel like I was a charity case. People who were supposed to be my family did not want me."

Sarah's heart squeezed a little at the words. "That is so very sad. I don't have it easy here but I don't think my situation can be compared to yours. You obviously had a very difficult childhood."

"You are older and very strong. It would have been nearly the same if you were as young as I was."

He was correct. Bella would do the smallest thing and Bernice would scold her. Just last night, her sister had begun eating the soup before everyone else and Bernice had spent over ten minutes rebuking her. Sarah constantly felt like the shield between her sisters and her aunt.

She released a long slow breath, and looked up at Mr. Arbusson. He was wearing a rather satisfied expression on his face. That was when she realized what he had done. He had asked her a question and she had refused to answer; then he had shared some personal information with her and without realizing it, she had given him an answer.

Sarah was impressed, but she was also wary.

"That was cleverly done, Mr. Arbusson. You shared

something about yourself to entice me to do the same. Do you always manipulate people this way?"

He shook his head. "It is not manipulation, my lady. It is simply psychology."

She inclined her head and regarded him. She quite liked him, and not because of his looks or the way he made her cheeks heat and her heart rate speed up. He was intelligent and very much aware of the world around him. And she had just discovered that they shared something in common. They were both orphans who knew what hardship was like.

"I still cannot accept your compliment," she reminded him. "And I would prefer it if you stopped visiting."

Any other man would have looked affronted, but he remained placid, amused even. "Very well," he drawled after what seemed like a long pause. "I will not visit the house anymore if that will help you keep peace in your life. But would you like to take a walk with me tomorrow?"

Her lips parted in preparedness to refuse, but the words froze in her throat. He was a very persistent man.

"Why do you insist?" she asked him, truly wanting to know.

"Because you have struck me, Lady Sarah."

"Quit being ridiculous, Mr. Arbusson—"

"Tamworth," he corrected. "Call me Tamworth."

She laughed. "You are very daring, aren't you? You ask me to walk with you when I am trying to get you out of my home, and now you want me to address you by your Christian name?"

"One must be daring when dealing with a woman like you," he grinned.

Sarah shot to her feet, her heart flipping over and over in her chest. "That is enough, Mr. Arbusson. If you are not going to leave, then I will leave you."

Tamworth…

Tamworth? Was she already addressing him as Tamworth in her mind? He rose to his feet then, still grinning.

"I will do as you wish, my lady," he said.

Be calm, my heart. Sarah breathed slowly as she nodded.

He took a step toward her and leaned forward so his mouth was close to her ear. "You have not seen the last of me," he murmured, his deep low voice sending shivers all through her.

"Goodbye, Mr. Arbusson," she whispered.

"Tamworth," he corrected, and then left.

For several weeks afterward, Tamworth was constantly on Sarah's mind. When she woke in the morning, she thought of him, wondering where he could be and what he might be doing. During the day when she was busy working on a dress, he would creep into her thoughts and she would find herself pausing, taking a moment to dream a little.

Lisa had sulked around the house, giving Sarah the cold shoulder after Tamworth had ignored her, but she had ripped a dress at an event and needed Sarah to mend it for her. So she had returned to being all sweet. The things people did…

On this fateful afternoon, Sarah decided to take a walk on Boston Common. Millie had been in a mood after yet another rebuke from Bernice, and Sarah had offered a walk. Millie had declined, opting to take a nap instead. Bella had also opted to nap and Sarah decided to go by herself. She didn't take walks as often as she liked because of her work, so this day felt almost special. It was now late summer and the busy streets bustled with color and life. She loved the energy and the color.

That thought prompted her to look down at her gray dress. How much longer until she could go back to her usual attire? Her father had now been gone eight months. She looked like she was still mourning, but her heart was too full of her father's betrayal to allow herself to grieve at all. Many people had arrived with claims that he owed them money, but only those with proof had been attended to by her. She had collected all the details and promised to pay them. Somehow, it had fallen to her rather than Landon, who had shirked paying anything to anyone. She did not blame him. The burden was not his to bear. It was not hers either, but he'd been her father. So, what was she to do?

She had decided to begin repaying each debt once her shop was established. At that thought, she smiled and looked up at the clear cerulean sky. She was very close to achieving her goal.

"I didn't know phantoms took walks in parks," a deep voice intoned from behind her.

She did not need to look to know who it was. That voice had occupied quite a bit of space in her thoughts and she had played it over and over again.

"I didn't know a shadow I thought dismissed has turned up once again to follow me," she replied.

Tamworth fell into step beside her. "Good afternoon, Lady Sarah," he greeted.

She kept her face lowered for a moment, not wanting him to see how excited she really was to meet him again. That knowledge would ruin her act of nonchalance. "Good afternoon, Mr. Arbusson."

"You still insist on addressing me so formally."

"Why should I not? I know how you work, now. Once I step over the threshold into informality, you will insert yourself more into my life."

"I am not inserting myself against your will, though, am I?" The amusement in his voice had disappeared.

She decided to turn and look at him then, and her breath caught in her throat. Not only was he better looking than she remembered, but he was regarding her with something strange in his eyes. Something like longing. She laughed inwardly. Why would a man like him want someone like her?

A plain, debt-ridden orphan.

"If you don't want to see me again, just say so and I will leave for good."

A part of her wanted him to leave. She felt if she didn't see him again, she would be able to stop herself from falling for him. But the other part of her desperately wanted him to remain.

"I am not going to answer that," she mumbled and continued walking.

"A neutral response. You want to respond in the positive but fear you will appear vulnerable. But you certainly do not want to respond in the negative." He reached out and took hold of her elbow, pulling her to a stop.

They were under a tree that shaded them from the late afternoon sun as the gentle summer breeze rustled the leaves.

"Sarah," he said softly, like the whisper of the wind, and then he smiled, no doubt at her expression of surprise. "I prefer to call you Sarah. It is too pretty a name for me not to use it."

"What do you want?" she asked.

"Is it not obvious?"

She turned away. "I can't."

"You mean, you won't."

"Yes. I won't. Protecting my sisters is the most important thing in the world to me. I don't have room for romance right now. Please understand that, Tamworth."

He reached out and tucked an escaped lock of hair behind her ear. "If I had any intention of leaving before, which I did not, then you have changed my mind by calling me by my name."

"I didn't mean to…"

"The heart speaks for itself, does it not?"

Sarah huffed out a breath. "You are insufferable."

"And you are intriguing," he drawled.

"There you go, flirting with me again." She left the shade and began walking toward a nearby gazebo.

He followed her. There was no getting rid of him. "You know, life seems to work in very peculiar ways, sometimes. You denied me a walk once, and yet here we are."

"That is because you have been following me. You forced life's hand."

He laughed. "Sarah, I am a very busy man. I cannot afford to sit in front of your house every day, hoping to catch you when you come out for a walk."

"You may have stationed someone to watch me."

"And you think they will get the message to me and at such short notice I will arrive in time. Barely minutes after the start of your walk?"

Tamworth was a very interesting man and he made her think. He provoked her mind. "All right. You win," she conceded.

"What exactly did I win?"

"This argument."

He made a disappointed face. "I thought I had won something more valuable than a mere argument. Alas, I may have to try again."

She chuckled, trying to tamp down a stronger laugh. "You are unbelievable."

"So are you." His voice had taken on that sensual thrum again.

"I should head home." Yes, it was time to cut this walk—this marvelous walk—short. Sarah had to do something to resist him.

"Allow me to accompany you." He offered her his arm.

"No!" She yelped the word, then realized how odd she must have sounded. She sucked in a deep breath and then repeated in a more even tone. "No, thank you."

"You still don't want to be seen with me."

She pasted a smile on her face. "Goodbye, Mr. Arbusson." Then she turned and scurried off as fast as she could down the path.

CHAPTER TEN

Two months later, Sarah secured the lease on a shop in Newbury Street, Back Bay. It was where the Boston elite shopped and one of the best locations for a dressmaking business in the city. She named her shop *La Robe Dorée,* not because it was French and people associated the language with sophistication and good fashion—though that was an unexpected bonus—but because this was part of a golden dream. The dream to earn her freedom. If she were ever to be rid of all her burdens, she would prance in a golden dress and declare her freedom to the world. Hence the name.

Once the shop was open, she raised the price of her dresses. Maintaining a shop in Newbury Street was not cheap and she had debts to begin paying. She was not afraid that it would slow her business. Her clients would receive top quality service, and top quality commanded a high price, always.

Sarah had not seen nor heard from Tamworth since their walk in the park. To cope, she had immersed herself in her work and kept busy.

She was preparing to close the shop and go home when she heard a knock on the door. She peeked through the window and her traitorous heart jumped with joy. For there he was, dressed in black, as usual.

She unlocked the door and inclined her head to greet him. He moved his hands from where they had been hidden under his coat, to reveal a bottle of wine and two glasses.

"We need to celebrate," he said, holding them up.

She stepped away from the door and allowed him to enter, beaming. When she closed the door and turned around, she found him regarding her with that enigmatic look in his eyes.

"My felicitations," he said. "You never told me you were planning to open a dress shop. I did not even know you designed dresses."

"You were too busy pestering me to walk with you," she returned. She wanted to ask him where he had been for the past two months but restrained herself. Appearing too eager wouldn't do her any good. For all she knew, he only found her intriguing because of her plight.

Tamworth set the glasses down on a side table that held a small gilt mirror and poured wine into each before offering her a glass. She accepted it gladly and took a satisfying sip. He began to look around the shop with assessing eyes.

"It still needs work," she said, feeling she had to defend how the place looked. Most shops on the street had quality furnishings, but hers still had just the basics. It looked incomplete, but she loved it, nevertheless.

"It doesn't matter," he said. "One starts slow and builds up. That was how I started. A small bar that grew into a bigger one which then became a club. One club became two, and so on…" He was smiling down at her.

"That is inspiring."

"I am happy I can inspire." He finished his wine and set the glass down. "How are you, Sarah?"

She was happy. She still had a long way to go but she was proud of herself for coming this far and persevering. *La Robe Dorée* had given her hope, and that was a precious thing.

"I am content," she said to him.

He stepped forward. "I can tell. The shadows in your eyes have lessened and your smile appears more readily."

She smiled again, proving him right.

"I have something for you," he said, reaching into his pocket and pulling out a small black velvet box. Tamworth held it out to her.

"What is this?" she asked, suddenly anxious.

"Open it and find out."

Very slowly, she opened the box, and lying on the satin interior was a brooch. Her breath caught at the magnificence of it. It was a small golden dress; the bodice was covered with tiny topaz stones and the skirt with a scattering of diamonds. The diamonds looked like the sparkle a golden dress might have under the light.

A half laugh, half gasp escaped her at the sight. "Tam…" She was unable to complete his name.

"Yes?" He looked delighted at her reaction, and very proud of himself.

"I can't accept this," she breathed. "It is too much. It is too beautiful."

"And you think you don't deserve beautiful things?"

"Not something as expensive as this. This cost a small fortune, clearly."

"And it is yours."

Sarah looked up at him. "What does this mean, Tamworth?"

"I see you speak my name freely now. You even said *Tam* earlier, which I found rather endearing."

"I was speechless!" she defended. "And you are changing the subject. What does this mean? What do you want for it in return?"

When a man gave a woman a present such as this, it was not without expectation of something in return. She was a respectable woman and he was no cad, but he was not courting her either. So what exactly *did* he want?

"Don't give it any meaning. Just see it as a gift from one friend to another."

"Are we friends?"

"Aren't we?" His voice was soft.

"I still don't understand," she said.

"Sarah," he chuckled, "just accept the brooch and stop over-thinking it."

"Thank you," she breathed.

He gave her a nod and turned to the wine on the side table. "Share one more glass with me?"

She nodded, feeling overcome. He offered her another glass of the red liquid and she took a sip.

"When I heard the shop was called *La Robe Dorée*, I thought this brooch appropriate. You can wear it every day, and anyone who sees it will be reminded of this place. And I do have French origins, you know."

She did recall him saying something along those lines once, but it occurred to her that she didn't actually know a lot about him. Well, they had not met many times but still… He was rather mysterious. He only let her know what he wanted her to know. And he had not defined their relationship beyond friendship, which she found odd. She believed there could be something romantic between them; indeed he had seemed to imply it when they were at Boston Common, but he always managed to confuse her.

"Do you have family still in France?" she asked him.

Tamworth only shook his head and collected the brooch from her hand, then reached just below her shoulder and lifted the fabric of her gray dress to pin it there. He stepped away from her and assessed the result.

"It looks beautiful," he said.

Sarah swallowed, trying as hard as she could to slow her heartbeat. She looked down at her arms and found goosebumps all over her skin.

"Come, you should get home. I am sure your sisters will be anxious to see you."

She agreed to accompany him in his carriage. On their way to Bernice's house, she kept looking down at her brooch every time they passed a street lamp.

"I am happy you like it," he murmured.

"I am happy I have it," she returned.

"There is something I have been wondering about for some time now," he said. Sarah could not see his face well in the dark interior of the carriage and was unable to discern his expression. She felt somewhat at a disadvantage just then. "Why do you have to work?"

Surely, he was joking. "Are you seriously asking that?"

"Yes."

"Are you telling me that you really haven't heard about the debts my father left me with?"

"I know of the debts, of course, but I thought your cousin would take them on. You are a genteel lady, not someone a gambler's debt should weigh down."

She turned away from him and starerd out the window. "My cousin is not inclined to pay them, so it falls to me."

"But that is not right. It is not fair."

"Well, tell that to the man who placed this burden upon me in the first place. My father. He found a way out and left his children homeless. If Bernice had not offered to shelter us, my sisters and I would have been on the streets."

"No, you would not have been on the streets, Sarah. You are too resourceful and determined to ever have allowed that. You would have done everything in your power to make sure your sisters were protected. I know you, Sarah."

She slowly turned her head in his direction. She didn't know whether or not he could see her face, but she didn't care. Because, in that moment, she was as certain of the fact as she was of the heart beating in her chest, that she was in love with Tamworth Arbusson. He had reached into the deepest part of her heart and stoked the embers there.

Perhaps he could see what she was feeling, and perhaps not, but he reached out and took her hand, gently stroking the back of it with his thumb.

"I can provide you a house to move into with your sisters," he offered.

Sarah was touched by his generosity but shook her head. He had just gifted her a very expensive brooch. She couldn't possibly accept more from him. Besides, she would much prefer to take care of the girls by herself without anyone else's help. She had just proven to herself—and obviously also to Tamworth—that she was capable.

"I have found a small townhouse in South End that I plan to move us to. I just needed to get the store up and running first," she informed him.

"You want to do this by yourself?" he asked.

She nodded, and he tightened his grip on her hand a little. "If you ever need help, remember I am here."

She nodded again and he released her hand and leaned back against his seat.

When they reached Bernice's house, he took her

hand again, and this time, he raised it to his lips and kissed her knuckles, one by one. The sensation gave her butterflies in the stomach.

"I'll see you soon," he murmured.

Seven weeks later

SARAH LINGERED IN FRONT OF THE DRAWING ROOM doorway feeling somewhat anxious. Her relationship with Bernice had deteriorated since the establishment of *La Robe Dorée*. Sarah had stopped paying her when she opened the store and her aunt had not been happy about it. She had demanded Sarah pay for staying in the house but Sarah had instead informed her aunt that she and her sisters would soon be leaving.

Bernice had become harsher on her sisters, to the point where Sarah had had to take Bella with her to work. The youngest of her cousins, Portia, was a year older than Bella and had been bullying her. Instead of Bernice putting a stop to it, she encouraged the poor behavior.

Taking a deep breath, Sarah walked into the drawing room. "Aunt Bernice," she began.

"Come to tell me that you are finally leaving?" the woman said in a derisive tone.

"Yes," she admitted. "I have found a house and everything is set."

Bernice was reclining on the sofa and she slowly sat

up. "Tell me something, Sarah. What respectable lady rents a house and lives there by herself? Have you no care for your reputation?"

Sarah's back went rigid at Bernice's words. "I will be living with my sisters, not alone."

"Your sisters are Landon's wards!" Bernice snapped.

Keeping her voice as even as possible, Sarah countered. "You will not stop me from taking my sisters with me. I only came to inform you that we are leaving and to thank you for your generosity."

"Landon is their legal guardian, not you."

Sarah's temper rose, despite her best efforts. "I don't give a damn who their legal guardian is. I have cared for those girls for years, ever since my mother passed, and no one is separating us. No one!"

Bernice stood. Sarah knew what she was doing. She had been defeated but had refused to accept it, so she wanted to make Sarah pay by trying to keep the girls and threatening her with the law.

"Landon can take you to court for this."

Sarah scoffed. "He can try. Landon is not interested in carrying their responsibility. Besides, he cannot take me to court. He cannot spare the money."

"How dare you!"

Landon was a heavy gambler just like her father had been, and if he did not stop, he would likely find himself in a rut he was unable to get out of.

"After all I have done for you!"

"And I thank you for everything you have done for

me, and for my sisters." With that, Sarah turned around and stalked out of the room.

She met her sisters in the foyer. Their cloaks were on and their bags had already been placed in the hire carriage. They were ready to start a new life in their new home. She held out her hands to Bella and Millie and together they walked out of the house.

Bella and Millie had not yet seen the new townhouse, but Sarah had spent the better part of a week arranging it properly and making it a home for her sisters. Tamworth had even sent her something for the house—a lovely Chinese vase. She decided it would decorate the tiny front hall.

Sarah looked out the carriage window as they approached the house and her excitement grew. "We are here!" she declared.

The two girls looked out to see their new home. "Which one is it?" Millie asked.

"The red-brick house with the peonies and gardenias in front," Sarah replied, grinning.

"Oh, it's lovely!" Bella breathed.

Yes, it was a lovely house. It was small, much smaller than anything they were used to, but it was theirs. Sarah had signed the papers to ensure they could stay for several years. The carriage stopped in front of the house and there was a bit of a struggle between Millie and Bella to get out of the carriage first. Sarah pulled Millie back by the sash of her dress to allow Bella down first. Millie moaned, "It's not fair!"

Sarah had a surprise waiting for them in the house

and she could hardly wait for them to find out what it was. She took the lead and guided them up the stone steps to the front door and knocked. One of the surprises opened the door for them.

"Cooper!" Bella screamed and jumped into his arms.

Then the other surprise appeared behind him and this time it was Millie who ran forward and into their housekeeper's arms. "Mrs. Fowler!"

When they had lost their former house, all the servants had been dismissed, but Sarah had promised Cooper and Mrs. Fowler that the moment she could, she would have a place for them. When she had rented this house, she had called them back and both had arrived promptly. They were practically family, too.

They entered the house and the girls ran through every room, exploring.

"Well done, Sarah," Mrs. Fowler said. "You did all of this in just a year. It is remarkable."

Another good thing coming their way was the end of their mourning period. They would soon be able to wear colorful dresses and Sarah had been working on that for some time.

CHAPTER ELEVEN

Several months later

Sarah's relationship with Tamworth grew, but not in the conventional way. It was still somewhat unclear if what they had was romantic or not. It was somewhere between romance and friendship. She sometimes felt he was holding back and didn't understand why.

But she was happy with just having him in her life. And yes, she was in love with him. Most women would wish for their feelings to be returned or even for him to offer marriage, but oddly enough, Sarah did not have those thoughts. She had written marriage off since losing their home and making the decision to do things on her own terms, and although she would have loved to know if Tamworth loved her in return, her mind was focused on taking care of her sisters.

Business had grown, to the point that she had taken

on an assistant, Camilla. Life was finally beginning fall into place for them all.

Tam had never been to their house, and she had never asked him why. As a matter of fact, her sisters knew nothing about him. She had not seen the point in telling them. Her friends Libby and Anna, however, knew a little.

He did spend quite a bit of time with her in her shop. She never knew quite when he would visit, but it was always at a time when no one else was in attendance, toward the end of the day. She could close the shop to the public and they would spend an hour together before he would give her a ride back home in his carriage. There was no particular pattern and thus his visiting times were unpredictable.

Like now…

Sarah had just turned the card on the door that read "closed", when a knock sounded on the door. She didn't peek through the window. She just assumed it was Tam and opened the door. Instead, she found a strange man standing there. Before she could ask him what he wanted, he handed her a sealed envelope.

"It is a message from the Raven," he said.

"The Raven?" she repeated, confused.

"Yes, ma'am."

She looked down at the envelope and the man quickly left. She closed the door and turned the key in the lock, feeling most unsettled. Who on earth was the Rave? She lifted the seal with her fingernail and opened the envelope. It was an invitation to a ball. A ball being hosted by Lady De LaFontaine. The invitation was addressed to her. But the messenger had said the missive was from the Raven. She shrugged, assuming the Raven was someone from the De LaFontaine household.

There was a note attached to the invitation:

Sarah,

I intended to deliver this invitation to you in person, but something came up in one of the clubs. I wish to attend this ball with you and shall pick you up on the night of the event. If that is all right with you?

Tam.

A feeling deep inside told her that something wasn't right. Of course, she would love to attend a social function with Tam, but why had he intercepted her mail? He could have just allowed it to be delivered to her home and then asked her the next time he visited; after all, the ball was still a week away.

And the messenger had called him the Raven.

The following day

TERRANCE READ WAS THE MAN WHO SUPPLIED SARAH with Belgian lace. Besides the monthly deliveries of lace, he also supplied beads and a bit of town gossip. So, when he came to make a delivery, Sarah decided to solve the mystery that had deprived her of much-needed sleep last night.

"Mr. Read," she called as he was about to leave.

"Yes, my lady?"

"Do you know anyone by the name of the Raven?"

"Ah, yes. He owns The Barbican and I supply him with the finest French brandy."

"Tamworth Arbusson?"

Mr. Read was quiet for a moment as though he did not know that name. After a moment, he shrugged. "Yes, I think that is his proper name. Everyone in town calls him the Raven."

How had she not known that Tam had a moniker more well-known than his own real name?

"What…" She swallowed to moisten her throat that had suddenly gone dry. "What kind of man is he?"

Mr. Read laughed nervously and something heavy dropped to the pit of her stomach. "I am not sure how to answer that. I mean…the man is a mystery. People hardly see him unless they enter the club and when he is out, he is always dressed in black."

"Is he a good man?"

"He has never gone out of his way to cause trouble, but word on the street is he will not hesitate to punish anyone who crosses him. His clubs have game rooms and many of these fancy gentlemen go there to gamble away their fortunes. It is said that he never forgives a debt. And why should he?" Mr. Read shrugged again. "He is just running a business."

The more Terrance Read told her, the more she

realized she did not know Tam one bit. He hadn't necessarily portrayed himself as someone different but he hadn't been altogether truthful with her, either. The word on the street may be false a lot of the time, but there was always an element of truth. As much as she didn't want to believe Terrance Read, he had no reason to lie.

"I made a delivery sometime last year and I heard talks in hushed whispers. A man owed him money worth a grand house, and not the small houses in town. A mansion. Apparently, the man took his own life to avoid paying the debt, and left three daughters. He was some earl, I think. I didn't get any names. I don't know if the Raven ever forgave the debt given the man was dead."

Sarah's heart couldn't seem to make up its mind whether to go into super-fast mode, or stop altogether. She felt ill.

Mr. Read did not need to give her any names. She knew who that man had been. And he had been in debt to the *Raven*? To *Tam* himself?

"Thank you, Mr. Read," she said, anxious for him to leave now. "Do have a good day."

"You too, my lady."

She closed the door after him and slumped against it. She felt like a knife had been plunged into her body and was being cruelly twisted. Everything Tam had told her was based on a lie. The late Earl Waelcombe owed Tam a great deal of money, and he had never mentioned it to her.

"Are you all right, Sarah?" Camilla asked, entering

the room. She had been in the back storeroom unpacking some of their deliveries.

"I just feel a little faint. Can you take care of things for a while?"

Camilla nodded with alacrity and Sarah moved through the back storeroom and into a smaller secluded room that she used as an office. She sat behind a small desk, her thoughts going round in useless circles. How was she going to handle this? She did not even know where to start…

Since his visiting times were unpredictable, Sarah sent word to The Barbican asking him to come at closing time this evening. She had also sent a message to her home, to let her sisters know she was working late and to dine without her this evening.

She had done a lot of thinking during the afternoon, and decided to give him a chance to provide some answers. She would confront him, but not in a confrontational manner. It was time for truth instead of evasion or downright lies.

After Camilla left for the day, Sarah sat on the settee and waited. The hour he usually visited passed and he did not show. Still she waited. Finally, two hours later, there was a knock. She opened the door and there he was.

For the first time since they had known each other, he looked strained. Could he already know that she had discovered his lies? Sarah kept as blank an expression on her face as she could, so that he wouldn't suspect a thing.

"Forgive my lateness," he said, stepping into the shop. "There was an accident yesterday in one of the clubs, Paragon, and it took a lot of time sorting things out."

She didn't say anything. He regarded her dubiously, but then concern took over. "Are you all right? You asked to see me."

"Tam, what name does the town know you by?" she asked coolly.

"The Raven," he replied.

"How did I not know about it?"

"You never asked."

"Very well. How much does my father owe you?"

Most men who cared would blanch at that question. The Raven's face only hardened and the sudden coldness in his gaze shut her out. "How did you know?"

"It doesn't matter how I found out. Did you ever plan to tell me?"

"Yes."

"When?"

"When I was sure you would be ready."

"On what grounds are you making that determination?" Anger leached through her. Every plan to handle this thoughtfully had been stomped on by her ire. He had lied to her and he had betrayed her.

"Sarah, I need you to understand that I did not mean—"

"That day you came to pay condolences," she cut him off. "What exactly had you come to do?"

His sharp green eyes narrowed and his strong jaw firmed. "You really want to know?"

"Tell me!"

"I came to inform you of the debt that was owed to me by your father. But I pitied your circumstances, and decided to delay breaking the news to you."

A bitter laugh almost choked her. "You pitied me." Her voice was so brittle it sounded like it could shatter at any moment.

He took a step toward her. "Sarah—"

Her hands shot out with her palms facing forward to stay him. "Don't come near me. Now, tell me how much my father owed you."

Tamworth revealed the figure and her knees buckled under her. She began to fall. He reached out in time to grab her but she struggled out of his grasp and staggered back until she landed on the settee. How was she ever going to pay him that amount? She looked up at him then and didn't recognize the man in front of her. There was not an ounce of sympathy in his face. Every inch of him looked like he had been carved from stone.

"And you won't forgive it, will you?"

"It is not that simple."

"Gambling is like an ailment, so why do you allow it?" she asked.

"It's business," he replied. "It is not my fault that those who lose have no discipline."

Sarah's eyes widened. This man had no heart! "And you cannot forgive even when a man is dead?"

"Took his own life," he corrected. "He wanted to force my hand. Make me forget the debt he owes me."

Maybe that was the reason her father had killed himself. Maybe he had thought the debts would be forgiven in the event of his death. But Sarah doubted that. The bank documents she had signed when they had come to take the house had proven that he knew death would not erase a debt. "That's not true," she said, trying to convince herself more than him. "And why should I have to be the one to pay? The debt is not mine."

""It is the way of things. The debt *is* yours, now, as the eldest child. Especially as your cousin will not honor it." He sounded sorry but he did not look it. "It's sad that we don't get to choose our parents," he added softly.

That sealed it. The pain she had felt when her father had taken his life was nothing compared to the pain wringing her insides in that moment. It would have hurt her less if he had just told her on the first day they had met. But no, he had to first make her fall in love with him, then allow her to find out the truth from someone else, before he finished her off by telling her he could never forgive such a debt.

Tamworth Arbusson was a twisted genius, well-versed in the art of inflicting the worst emotional pain imaginable. Suddenly, the walls around her began to close in and the feeling of suffocation reared itself. Her golden dream began to dissipate into nothing but gray dust.

"Get out," she rasped, barely able to breathe.

"Sar—"

"Get out, you vile monster!" she screamed at him.

Tam turned on his heels and walked out of *La Robe Dorée.*

The following day

DESPITE KICKING HIM OUT OF HER SHOP YESTERDAY, Sarah found herself the following evening at The Barbican. She had been informed by the steward he was in, and waited while he checked with his master. A few minutes later, she was being led through one of the darkest establishments she had ever set foot in to his office.

Hardly any natural light made its way into the room. All that illuminated the place were dim amber lights from sconces on the walls. The walls were covered with dark wood and the carpeting was in shades of brown, dark blue, and occasionally dark green.

His office was even worse.

When Sarah had woken that morning…or rather, when she had gotten out of bed that morning after a night without sleep, she wished she had dreamed everything up. The man she thought she knew was kind and considerate, gentle, and caring. He even had a good sense of humor. But the man before her was the exact opposite. This was obviously the real man. The Raven. The other—Tamworth—had merely been a tool to torment her, destroy her trust and faith in people even more than it already had been.

He was standing behind an incredibly large mahogany desk with his back to the draped windows. He was almost completely shadowed, and she could not see his expression properly. Was this not what the devil did? Pull her into his den and expose her while he continued to conceal himself?

She marched forward and when she was in front of the desk, she gently laid down the folded sheet of paper she had brought with her.

"This is an undertaking. The one you probably have was signed by my father. This one has my signature on it and you can hold me to it. I will pay you."

Not giving him a chance to answer, she turned and stalked to the door, her back ram-rod straight. But when she reached the door, she remembered something else. Reaching into her reticule, she pulled out a black velvet box and walked back to the desk where—with shaking hands—she placed it on top of the folded document before leaving.

CHAPTER TWELVE

Present day

Tam rolled the golden dress brooch between his fingers as he sat behind his desk, remembering the past and unable to concentrate on work.

Meeting Sarah's sisters for the first time today had affected him more than it should have, reminding him of the reason he had stayed away all these years. Bella was a delight to be around and Millie was sweet and rather earnest. And Sarah… His hand closed over the brooch, squeezing it tight.

A knock sounded on his office door and he called for whoever it was to come in. Nate appeared in the doorway. From his expression, Tam knew the man did not have any news for him. Living on the streets the way he had after he left the family, Tam had learned to read people, their actions, and what their expressions meant.

Once he had the means to purchase books, he had taken to devouring anything he could find on human behavior. Something in him craved to understand people and their motives. Perhaps he felt it would help him understand his own family and why they had sent him away.

He remembered Sarah once implying that he manipulated people. He did, he supposed. By reading them, he found ways they could be useful to him. He had made a critical mistake with her, however.

"Do you have anything for me, Nate?" He asked the question anyway, already knowing the answer. He looked down at the golden dress brooch between his fingers after Nate shook his head.

"More time will be needed."

"Take more time then. Go find out more."

Nate left and Tam stood. It was time to call in a favor. A visit was warranted to one of those members of high society he had gotten close to; one of those who ought to be a friend but were only regarded as acquaintance because they weren't sure about the Raven and his reputation.

Retrieving his coat from a rack, he draped it over his shoulders and headed out. He was halfway down the hall when an urge stopped him in his tracks. He traced back his steps until he was once again behind his desk. He turned to face the window and then raised his hand to pull the drapes apart, hanging them on gilded hooks on either side of the window frame.

Taking a step back and turning around, he surveyed

the office, noting how the incoming light changed the place. It was an intimidating room only when the curtains were drawn together. When they were open, one could almost see the beauty of the room. Of course, it had not been designed with beauty in mind. It had been designed to cast trepidation over whoever was brave, or foolish, enough to venture in.

Still, it looked better with the drapes open, he concluded.

When he met Mr. McGuire on his way out, he ordered the curtains in specific places throughout the club to be opened. Mr. McGuire looked at him as though he had gone mad, but agreed to have the task carried out, nevertheless.

He gave his carriage driver the address of a home and climbed in. Social calls had never been something he did unless absolutely necessary. Like now. His eyes sought out the spot Sarah had sat in earlier and thought he caught something on the seat. He moved over to take a closer look and found a black bead. She'd had a black-beaded reticule with her. This must have come off it.

Tam picked it up and examined it, holding the bead up to the sunlight streaming into the carriage. If he were a collector of Sarah's lost things, he would place this into his breast pocket. And he did. Just like the golden dress brooch.

What would she say if she saw that golden dress again? Would she remember the day she had returned it? He didn't think she would ever forget. Her continued dislike of him—stemming from that day—was obvious.

How would she react if she knew that he kept remembering that day, too?

The carriage slowed and then stopped, pulling him out of his ponderings. He climbed down and walked to the door where he knocked and was subsequently granted entry. He was led to a salon. The same salon in which he had sat with Sarah when he made himself comfortable by reaching for a decanter of brandy. He did the same again now, pouring the liquid into two snifter glasses.

"Raven!" A stentorian voice boomed and a small smile tilted Tam's lips before he turned. "Honestly, when Quentin informed me you were here, I thought I was dreaming."

"Come now, Belleville, this is not the first time I have visited."

"I didn't think you would return after Dianne chased you away last time." Rupert came fully into the room and Tam proffered him a glass of his own liquor.

"I was here at the engagement ball."

"So you've only begun to return now you're certain Dianne is taken!"

Tam quirked a smile and shrugged. Rupert's sister, the popular Lady Dianne, had once had her eye on him and when he would visit Rupert, she would insert herself in situations to gain his attention. One evening she had unabashedly flirted with him, and then tried to kiss him when she thought they were alone. Luckily, Rupert had seen everything—including Tam's avoidance of his sister despite her best efforts—and Tam had left the house with his head still on his shoulders and the relationship with Rupert still existing.

That had been a year ago.

The men sat and Tam got straight to business. "This is not a friendly call, I must warn you," he said.

"Oh, from the time of day, I presumed as much."

"Good. I am looking for someone. A Mrs. Clara Hart."

"Are you actually asking for my help, Tamworth?" Rupert quipped, his eyes dancing.

"Don't start getting any ideas," Tam warned. "I am merely calling in a favor."

Rupert took a sip of his drink before setting the glass down on the center table in front of him and leaning forward. "That's the thing, Tamworth. You never call in favors. You are a man who ensures you need nothing from people. You owe no one anything, yet are owed a *lot*."

Tam made a show of rolling his eyes and looking bored. But deep inside, he knew Rupert was correct. He did avoid anything that might lead him to ask for help. It was the reason he had gotten to where he was in life, without being indebted to anyone.

"Are you done talking nonsense?" he asked.

Rupert leaned back. "Yes, quite."

"Then give me what I need. Help me find Clara Hart. She was last seen in Charlestown."

"The woman responsible for that affair involving the Armstrong-Leeds girl?"

"That's the one."

"Done," Rupert said. Tam knew this was not a hollow promise. The man had worked in the military in some kind of espionage capacity, and if there was anything he was good at, it was tracking people down.

"Thank you."

Rupert chuckled. "What are friends for?"

Friends.

Despite what Tam had said to Sarah, Rupert *was* more than an acquaintance. He was Tam's friend. He was generally unwilling to admit their closeness, even to himself, for fear of exposing vulnerability. People as intelligent as Sarah were intuitive enough to read such vulnerability if he let it show.

Tam downed his drink in one gulp and rose. "When should I expect information?"

"I will be in touch as soon as I have something."

He nodded. He trusted Rupert would find her, now that he had been provided with a name.

On the other side of town, Sarah and Libby sat in a carriage heading fast toward Charlestown.

"I'm so sorry, Sarah," Libby said with great feeling. She had just finished hearing the full tale of Sarah's love and betrayal by Tam. "The bits and pieces you let slip earlier to Anna and myself were bad enough, but this… How could he do this to you?"

It had been years, but Sarah was still raw. She had done everything she could to forget. And somehow, every day, something else reminded her of Tam and her broken dreams.

"Are you sure you and your sisters should be staying with him? He is a master manipulator."

"I did consider saying no, but the truth is, I do trust him with our safety," Sarah said.

"If you ever change your mind, you can all come stay with us. There is a lot of spare room at Armstrong-Leeds House."

Sarah smiled at her friend. "Thank you."

It was dark when they arrived in Charlestown. After they had disembarked near a police station, both women realized they did not know where to start.

"What is her full name again?" Sarah asked.

"Clara Hart, I think." Libby reached into her pocket and fished out a piece of paper. "Here, I have a drawing."

"Where did you get that?" Sarah was surprised but glad. She didn't know what Mrs. Hart looked like, and had been wondering how she would find someone without even knowing what they looked like.

"Ah. It is useful to have a fiancé who happens to be a private investigator."

They shared a quick grin.

"Was a location specified, regarding where the woman was last seen?" she asked Libby.

Her friend thought for a moment before shaking her head. "I don't believe so."

Sarah sighed. "All right. Might as well start there." She pointed toward the police station.

The building housing the station was old, and in Sarah's opinion should not be used as a police station. At the very least, it required some work to make it look less like it was about to fall down. Inside, they found a man behind a small counter. He was eating a sandwich and did not bother to look up at them when they entered.

"Good evening, Officer," Sarah greeted loudly. Libby only gave him a nod of acknowledgment when he finally looked in their direction.

"Evening, Miss," he replied, showing great disinterest in whatever they had come for.

"I am Lady Sarah Smith-Jones and this is Baroness Esk."

He blinked and set down the sad-looking half-eaten sandwich. "M-my ladies, what can I do for you?"

Libby took over. "Officer, I am certain you know of my case."

"Yes, yes, certainly. Everyone does."

"Good. I want to help. The murderer is still on the loose." She drew her brows together in a sad frown and made a show of looking distraught. "I am having nightmares because of it. I cannot rest until she is found and I want to help, Officer."

It seemed to work. The man looked like he felt sorry for Libby. "We are doing what we can, my lady."

"Thank you, Officer! Are you any closer to finding her?"

"We are still on it," he replied and Sarah tried not to roll her eyes. Of course, he was on the case, eating a sandwich instead of doing what he had been trained to do. "But why are you here in Charlestown? Shouldn't you be making such an inquiry at a station closer to your own residence?"

"We received word that she has been spotted here in Charlestown," Sarah said.

The officer blinked in surprise. "I never heard that. Where did you get such information?"

"Detective DeHavillend," Libby quickly put in.

"Oh. If it is from Detective DeHavillend, then it must be true."

"So, do you have anything for us?" Sarah asked.

He shook his head. "I am afraid not, my ladies, but rest assured that you will be informed as soon as we find her."

"Good. We shall take our leave then."

"Have a good evening."

Once they were out of the station, Sarah cursed out loud. She found the behavior and inefficiency of the police positively irritating, to say the least.

"Can you believe he did not even know she had been seen here?" Libby complained. "What exactly is his use, anyway?"

"To eat and look pretty," Sarah drawled, suddenly feeling tired.

Her words made Libby chuckle. "We should head home, Sarah. It is dark and we do not know this area well. I suggest we return tomorrow, but earlier in the day."

Sarah nodded. Coming here so late in the day had

not been the best idea, but at least she had started the search. When she saw Tamworth again, even though she wouldn't have anything new to tell him, she could at least honestly say she had taken some action.

Sarah had requested their carriage wait. Luckily the man had heeded her and they thankfully climbed aboard. They headed to Libby's home first.

"Promise me you will take care," Libby said before leaving the carriage.

"I promise," Sarah replied.

"I'll see you tomorrow."

"Of course."

Sarah yawned and stretched. She was truly tired and not just physically. The last two days had been exhausting in every way, courtesy of Tamworth. He could not have chosen a worse time to reappear in her life.

She returned to *La Robe Dorée* planning to ensure everything was locked up tight before heading to Raven Hall. She had left work without finishing everything she hoped to achieve that day. She was not going to do any work now, obviously, but she still felt the need to make sure things were organized; like the new designs she had sketched earlier. She didn't know if Camilla had put them away.

The carriage stopped and she paid the driver and disembarked before noticing a sleek black carriage right in front of the one she had hired. Tamworth.

Her stomach curled into knots as he stepped forward

to greet her. He had promised he would return in the evening, and here he was.

Sarah walked past him up the short steps to the door of her shop and rummaged through her reticule for the key. She noticed one of the beads missing but quickly dismissed the thought as she found the key.

Tamworth put his hand on her arm.

"Are you going to keep pretending I do not exist?" he asked softly.

CHAPTER THIRTEEN

He was very close to her. So close she caught his scent: rosewood and frankincense.

"You really should stop giving yourself more importance than you actually have." She was proud of the fact that her voice did not shake. She inserted the key in the lock and turned it.

"Where were you this evening?" He covered her hand on the door handle, freezing the action.

Sarah turned sharply. "Where was I?"

"Yes, I expected to find you here when I arrived over two hours ago."

She pushed the door and walked into the shop, and he followed on her heels. She took a taper and quickly lit a couple of the wall lamps. "Pardon me, but I don't have to report my every movement to you," she responded at last.

"I don't expect you to report to me, Sarah. I was just concerned."

She scoffed. "You? Concerned? If you were truly concerned, you wouldn't make me do this."

He released a frustrated breath and raked a hand through his hair. It was the first time she had seen him do such and it startled her.

"You agreed to it," he rasped.

"And you made me an offer I could not refuse!" She moved to the table she had been sketching on earlier, and began to gather the papers. Camilla, the good girl that she was, had left them untouched. She glanced over her shoulder at Tamworth. He sat on a settee and stared at her. "Well," she said. "Don't you look pretty, sitting there."

"Finish up and let's go home," he said in voice that was almost a growl.

Let's go home. Years ago, those words would have delighted her. She had dreamed of a home with him. Now the words were like empty shells being thrown at her. She took her time organizing the drawings. When she couldn't delay any longer and finally turned around, she found him sleeping. His head had fallen back, resting against the wall behind the settee, and his chest moved up and down rhythmically as he breathed.

She took a tentative step toward him, careful not to make any sound. Of its own volition, her hand reached out and stroked his dark silky hair. It was just as soft as she remembered. Her fingers moved down his temple to his cheekbone and then to his jaw. His eyelids, lined with long dark lashes, fluttered and she quickly withdrew her hand.

Her heart was beating fast in her chest and she placed her hand to it to calm it down. When he was not plotting and controlling people's lives, he looked peaceful, vulnerable even. Like now. Right now, he looked like the Tam she had fallen in love with. The Tam who had brought her happiness. The Tam she had lost.

But then again, he had never existed. Had he?

Sarah felt something touch her cheeks and when her fingers explored, she discovered tears. She quickly turned away and wiped them away with one of her gloves that she had discarded when she arrived. She reminded herself of the promise she had made to herself years ago. No one would make her feel vulnerable enough to cry. Then she turned around and called in as even a tone as she could muster.

"Tamworth, wake up."

TAM OPENED HIS EYES. HE HAD NOT BEEN SLEEPING AND thus, had felt everything overwhelming him. Today had been especially draining and while he waited for Sarah to finish organizing her drawings, he took a seat on the settee and leaned back to rest his eyes.

He was still awake when she finished and the sudden silence that fell in the room let him know that she was watching him. He could have opened his eyes, but the spell would be broken. He wanted the magic to continue, if only for a little while longer. *Her* magic. She snuck close and then stopped moving. Anticipation built inside him.

Soft fingers brushed his hair before gently raking through. The touch was tender, exploring, and it reminded him of when she used to do that in the past. Her fingers skimmed his temple on their way down, brushing his cheekbone and settling on his jaw. He wanted this moment to last forever and was contemplating raising his hand to hers to keep it in place but she suddenly stopped. He felt empty all over again.

He heard her step away, but could feel her eyes still watching him. A soft muffled sniff came, provoking him to feel an ache in his heart. An ache of his own making.

She called him to wake up and he opened his eyes. Before he got to his feet, he assessed her. Her posture was unusually rigid and tense.

What had happened just now? What had happened between them?

She opened the door and stepped out into the cold night and he followed. Instead of allowing her to lock the shop, he held his hand out for the key and when she placed it on his palm, her fingers brushed his, sending a rush of sensation through him.

Tam locked the door and passed the key back to her. This time, he held the keyring so their fingers didn't touch. But his effort not to touch her was rendered futile when it came time to hand her into the carriage. She wasn't wearing gloves, and as he held out his hand, part of him prayed she would refuse assistance.

But she did not. The confounding woman placed her hand in his.

"I was in Charlestown earlier," she said after the carriage had been set in motion. The lamps hanging on the outside of the carriage lit her face. He thought she looked extraordinarily beautiful.

He knew where she had been, because he'd had her followed. Before leaving The Barbican that morning to call upon Rupert, he had asked one of his men to surreptitiously watch over her. Nate had sent a messenger to inform him that she was in Charlestown shortly before she arrived back at the shop. Her search would have her looking in many neighborhoods, especially Charlestown and Roxbury, and he needed to keep her safe without physically being there himself.

"What did you find in Charlestown?"

"Nothing, actually. It was already dark when we—"

"We?"

"Baroness Esk and myself."

Now, that detail, he had not been told.

"Since she has encountered Mrs. Hart before, and happens to have a detective as a fiancé, I thought she could help me with some information. She insisted on accompanying me. We met a police officer there, but he didn't know anything. According to what Libby heard from Detective DeHavillend, Mrs. Hart has been spotted in Charlestown but when we got there, it was frustratingly too late to look. We will have to return."

He nodded, tempted to say that she had done well but he feared she might find it condescending. Instead, he reached into his breast pocket and retrieved the bead he had found earlier. He had saved it for this moment. An excuse to give her something.

"I believe you lost this earlier," he said, holding out the bead in the center of his palm. His now-gloved palm.

Her keen gray eyes widened. "Where did you find that?" she asked.

"In the carriage. It must have fallen while you were here this morning."

She collected it from him and smiled. "I noticed it was missing earlier and was rather discontented. I disliked the prospect of looking for a replacement bead."

He returned her smile. "And the reticule just does not look right without it, hmm?"

Her eyes narrowed and he guessed her mind was working out what to make of his statement.

"I am not being ironic, I promise."

"There simply is no telling with you."

"I could say the same about you," he returned, relaxing for the first time that evening. It was remarkable how they were able to shift from cordiality to intolerance and back again. They had harmony and disharmony at the same time.

"Why? I am not the one masking my intent and hiding my feelings."

"You think I hide my feelings?"

"Yes, and you do it very well."

She was not wrong. "You do not believe I have feelings, though."

She lifted a small shoulder. "I say that when I am not happy with you, which I have to admit is a lot of the time." She paused, her eyes searching his face. He tried to remain placid under the scrutiny. "But everyone has feelings, whether they want to admit them or not."

She suddenly yawned then and he found himself doing the same.

"What time is dinner served in Raven Hall?" she asked.

"Seven. Why?"

"What is the time?"

He reached into his vest pocket and pulled out a gold watch and flicked the lid open. "Half-past eight."

She settled back in her seat with an odd expression on her face.

"What is it? I assure you my household will not starve your sisters."

"They don't like to eat without me," she said. "And we are late."

A smile curved his lips fully then. Sarah was a woman with a large heart and she loved freely, unlike him. Despite her Aunt Bernice's unpleasantness, Sarah still visited her. What pained him the most right now was how tainted his image was in her heart. He was the only one, it seemed, that she could not forgive.

This was the one thing he wanted to correct most in his life. He had a chance now, but in order to do that, he had to keep her as close to him as possible. It was the reason he had suggested she move her sisters to Raven Hall when she had expressed concern for their safety. They would have been perfectly safe in their house in South End. He would have seen to that. But this option meant that Sarah remained close, and he could hopefully carry out his plan.

"Why are you smiling?" she asked him, curiosity in her gaze.

"Because I feel like it."

She lowered her eyes then and he knew why. Before their falling out, he had smiled often and every time he did, she became shy and lowered her gaze. He was very much aware of his charms on women, though no other woman's reaction moved him as deeply as Sarah's. Knowing that he made her flustered gave him a warm feeling deep inside.

"*You* made me smile," he admitted.

Sarah stopped smiling back at him. "Don't do this, Tamworth." She looked away. "Don't say such things to me."

Without thinking, he leaned forward and captured her chin with his fingers. He turned her face to his. "I have missed you, Sarah."

She closed her eyes as though to shut out his words.

"You may not have missed me and I don't blame you for that, but I want you to know that I *have* missed you." He inched his face closer to hers, dearly hoping—nay, praying—she would not reject his kiss like she had last night. When she did not make a move to draw away, he brushed his lips lightly against hers.

And that was when she pulled back.

It was a most painful torture. She still did not trust him. And Tamworth realized he still had a lot of work to do.

Raven Hall was quiet when they arrived at nine, but then again, the opulent manor was always quiet.

Tam had not said another word to her since she rejected his attempt to kiss her. He walked up the stairs behind her and she could feel his eyes on her. He made her self-conscious, to say the least.

As she reached the landing, footsteps thudded and Bella came running down the east wing stairs with Millie chasing her. Sarah knew that if the girls did not slow down, they would collide with her. She was unable to get out of the way in time and the inevitable occurred. Bella crashed into her and they tumbled in a heap to the floor.

"Oh," Millie said when she saw her sisters sprawled on the landing floor. "I didn't know you were back."

"Why did you not get out of the way?" Bella moaned. "We were having fun!"

Sarah pushed the younger girl off her as her ribs began to ache. She winced because her head hurt, too. So much for being worried the girls would miss her. They had just demonstrated that they were perfectly fine, and now her own body ached because of it.

Strong arms reached out and scooped her up. Tam's arms. Millie's gasp reached her ears and Bella sighed.

"I think I have hurt my arm," she said.

"Let me see," Millie said, taking Bella's arm and checking it.

Millie then shook her head. "No, you are just jealous Sarah is being carried by a handsome man."

Tam's chest shook as he chuckled, the sound creating a vibration in his chest that flowed into Sarah's body. "How about I come back for you after I carry Sarah to safety."

"Safety?" Bella asked, frowning petulantly. "What danger is there?"

"You," Tam and Millie said in unison.

Her sisters were exhausting and right now Sarah just wanted Tam to take her to her room so she could sleep her tiredness away. The camaraderie between Tam and her sisters did not escape her notice. No one would believe they had just met that morning.

Tam deftly kicked open the door to her assigned chambers and crossed to the sitting area where he lowered her onto one of the midnight blue sofas.

"Are you injured anywhere?" he asked with something like concern in his eyes.

"I was hit by a twelve-year-old girl, not a boulder. I did bump my head a little and my ribs." She couldn't wait to remove her corset. That would ease the ribs, surely.

"You should relax. I will have a maid bring up your supper and help you with a bath." He did not give her a chance to respond before he strode out of the room and pulled the door shut behind him.

A moment later, a maid walked in and curtsied. "I am June, sent to assist you, my lady."

Sarah sighed and rose from her chair to walk to the dressing room. "Could you please run a bath for me, June? And then help me undress."

She had not had the chance to explore her chambers earlier because she had been in a rush to leave, but as she looked around her dressing room, she took note of how tasteful the furnishings and fittings were. The colors might be dark but the quality was superb. That was no surprise as Tam always had the best.

Suddenly, she remembered the golden dress brooch he had given her and wondered what had become of it. She could ask him, but that would be revealing she still cared.

"Help me with these buttons, June," she said, indicating the back of her dress. The buttons ran from her collar down to the bustle and took some time to undo. Her ribs were still aching.

Oh, Bella! Dear child. What was she to do with the girl?

After her bath, she put on her nightdress and a satin robe. Millie and Bella were waiting for her when she exited the dressing room. They both wore impish smiles on their faces and Sarah grew suspicious.

"Sorry I crashed into you," Bella said, looking remorseful.

"It's all right. But know that until my rib stops aching, you will share your dessert."

She pouted. "That's not fair!"

"I rather think it is," Millie put in.

Sarah sat on the sofa adjacent to the one her sisters shared. "How was your day?"

Millie's blue eyes lit up. "This house is incredible! So many rooms to explore. Did you see the library?"

"And the gardens!" Bella supplied. "I wish you would stay home from work tomorrow so we could explore together."

Sarah wished that too, but between the dozen dresses she had to begin making, and Tam's quest which meant another trip to Charlestown, she would hardly have time to explore this magnificent manor.

"So do I," she whispered.

Her food arrived just then. She did not feel like eating at first, but the moment the food was unveiled, her mouth watered and she found herself reaching for the cutlery on the side of the tray and eating a bite of pheasant pie. The flavor filled her mouth, satisfied her senses, and brought a touch of warmth to her insides.

Sarah usually did not eat heavy meals this late, but tonight, she made an exception.

"So, tell us about Tamworth," Millie said, her blue eyes glittering with curiosity.

Sarah swallowed and took another bite. Then another, and then another…until she was halfway through the pie and could not eat any more of it.

"Keep eating," Millie drawled. "We are patient and we will wait. Won't we, Bella?"

Bella bobbed her head, causing her blonde curls to bounce. "Oh, definitely."

Sarah looked heavenward, sending up a silent prayer for grace from these girls. She ate half of the cherry cake dessert and offered the rest to her sisters. Millie declined but Bella ate with gusto.

"If I am getting married soon, I will have to maintain a trim figure," Millie said.

"Nonsense! Jace wouldn't mind if you look like a whale. He really likes you," Bella mumbled with her mouth half full.

"Stop talking with your mouth full, Bella," Sarah said automatically.

"Now that you have finished eating," Bella ignored her, "are you going to tell us about Tamworth?"

Generally, Sarah shared everything with the girls, but for some reason she was reluctant to talk about Tam. She decided to dodge their question by answering in a different manner. "Tamworth is in this house somewhere. I am sure you can find him and ask him yourself." She stood and approached the bellpull near the door. "Now, if you'll be so kind as to leave my room, I would like to get some sleep. Tomorrow is sure to be an incredibly busy day."

"Do you *like* Tamworth?" Millie asked, folding her legs under her on the sofa and placing a velvet pillow on her lap. She was making herself comfortable, essentially, instead of leaving the room.

"No, I don't like Tamworth." It was true. She did not like Tam. But she did love him. After all this time, she still loved him. Her heart had tried to deny it until that moment in *La Robe Dorée* when he had been asleep.

It had become undeniable then and her life was now further complicated. When she found his grandmother's necklace for him, she would return to her small house in South End and her busy life in Newbury while he would return to his life and forget about her once more.

She didn't want to think of how she would cope when that happened. He had tried to kiss her in the carriage and she had wanted him to. But she had pulled back in order to protect her heart from further hurt. To Tam, it was merely a whim, a simple desire. But to her, it was akin to a declaration of affection.

"But he likes you," Bella said.

"Well, that is not my problem and it certainly is not your business." Sarah crossed the sitting room and walked through the archway to her bedroom.

Fire crackled in the marble fireplace and her bed covers had been turned. She climbed under the covers and lay her head on the downy pillows. She had just closed her eyes when she felt a weight on her bed. Two weights, to be exact.

"Sarah, if ever you want to be with Tamworth, we support you," Millie said quietly.

"We mean it," Bella added. "He is a lovely man."

"You met him just this morning, girls. You don't really know who he is."

"But you do," said Millie, smiling.

Bella reached over and hugged her. "Good night, Sarah."

Millie didn't hug her but she gave her sister's hand a squeeze. "Night, Sarah."

"Goodnight, girls," she murmured.

Shortly after the girls left, she heard someone come in and clear the sitting room. Once the lights were doused and the door was firmly closed, she lay on her stomach and drew the covers over her head, trying not to cry.

CHAPTER FOURTEEN

Sarah flipped onto her back and sighed loudly, staring up at the ceiling. She must have been here for hours trying to sleep. Whenever she closed her eyes, she saw Tam's face. When she opened them, he was there in her mind. She could not get rid of him, and she could not sleep.

She raised her head to look at the clock on the dresser to her right. Three o'clock. She had been trying to sleep for more than four hours! Giving up, she threw back the covers and got out of bed. She reached for her satin robe and covered herself with it before padding across to the sitting room. She looked about the room, contemplating what to do with her time while sleeplessness was her companion.

Finding nothing interesting in her chambers, she opened the door and stepped out into the dark hallway. She went to Millie's door and opened it a little before poking her head in to check. Millie was asleep in her bed and her soft snores filled the room. She closed the door and moved to Bella's room, doing the same. The girl in the bed mumbled something incoherent, which brought a smile to Sarah's face.

Bella did tend to talk in her sleep. Very quietly, she closed the door and proceeded down the hall to the massive staircase. Her sisters had made mention of a library. Libraries usually occupied the first floor so she decided to check around and see if she could find it. Her feet were bare as she moved through the manor and the lush carpet felt luxurious beneath her feet.

All lights were off so she depended on moonlight filtering in from the windows to find her way.

When she reached the landing, she paused and looked up at Regina's portrait. The woman's emerald green eyes looked just like Tam's. He must have loved her very much to have her portrait in such a place.

What sort of childhood had he had? What had happened to shape him into the man he was now? What terrible thing had ripped his heart out of his chest and taken his conscience? She caught her breath and held it, before releasing a long, loud sigh. He was such an enigma.

She turned from the painting and went down the rest of the stairs to the grand foyer. She decided to explore through an archway she hadn't been yet. It looked like a library could be tucked away somewhere down the hallway. She arrived in front of two massive doors from which light streamed out at the base. Someone was in that room, and if her guess was correct, it would be none other than the brooding master of the house.

Part of her wanted to turn around and run back upstairs to her room. Another part urged her to place her hand on the door handle and turn it. Naturally, she listened to the voice that was against reason and opened the door.

Tam had his back to her. He was sitting in an armchair in front of the fireplace that burned gold in this late hour of the night. Every wall in the room was lined with floor-to-ceiling bookcases; each shelf filled with books. It would take her forever to read all the books in this room. It would take her forever to *find* a book in this place. The choices seemed nearly unlimited.

He must not have heard her come in, or else he was asleep. Either way, she closed the door quietly behind her and tentatively padded across the room to where he was seated. She was wrong. He was awake.

His hand moved and he set a glass containing a small amount of amber liquid down onto a glass-topped table beside him.

"I wonder what is keeping the lady awake at this late hour," he drawled.

"And I wonder why the gentleman is in a book heaven brooding at this late hour," she replied.

"I may have a malady."

"Oh? What sort of malady?" She moved to the armchair opposite his and sat in it, curling her legs under her and arranging her robe. This was anything but appropriate, and yet, she felt comfortable being there with him.

He did not respond but only lifted his glass from the table and downed the contents in one gulp, before rising and heading over to a table holding several decanters on top. Sarah studied him and the decanters from where she sat. None of them had any significant amount of liquor missing. He did not drink very much. She had always known that about him. Whenever he poured into a glass, he poured very small amounts. And she appreciated that.

Her father had imbibed far too much.

"Well, since you don't want to talk about your malady, then tell me about this library."

He turned to face her. "I told you my education stopped at twelve, right?" She nodded. "I have made books my companions to make up for that. Over the years, I have collected hundreds. When this library was built, I decided to multiply my collection. At least, I have something to read well into my old age."

"You certainly do." She stood and began walking around the grand library, her fingers skimming book spines as she went. "The girls were not exaggerating when they said this place was amazing. They loved it."

"I am happy they do."

One word from what he had just said caught her attention. "Are you happy, Tam? Or at least, a happy person?" She used his name deliberately, and saw a flicker of something in his eyes.

He stared at her for a long moment before

answering. "I am not. I have never been a happy person." He began to move toward her. Very slowly. "I don't know the woman who gave birth to me and she does not know me. She is married to an English baron. I do not even know if she has any other children. The only woman who ever cared about me was my grandmother, and she was taken from me when I was six. Then I lived with a horrible man until I turned twelve and escaped the house and the horror within."

He was standing in front of her now looking sad and forlorn. "Tam," she whispered, reaching out to stroke his jaw. He closed his eyes and turned his face into her palm, placing a soft kiss there. "You don't have to be alone."

"Do you know why I want that necklace found so desperately?"

She shook her head.

"It is one of the few items I have left of Regina's. I am not holding on to it for just the memory, for she is already with me in my mind, but it is something special." As he said *special*, he stroked her hair which was loose and cascading down her back. "Getting it back might bring me some happiness."

Heaven knew he needed some happiness, Sarah thought. She had come to understand something about him just now. He had only known love from one person, and it had been taken from him too early to understand it properly.

In the quiet of the night, she decided he deserved more than that. She did not expect anything in return, but if he could recognize and accept her love right now, then perhaps he would remember it for a very long time. Even though they were destined not to be together in the future, the memory might bring some light into his life when he needed it most.

She wrapped her arms around his neck and pulled him down into her arms. A sigh was drawn from him and he circled his arms about her waist and pulled her close, burying his face in the crook of her neck. Very gently, she stroked his hair and tried to show him as much comfort as she could.

They remained like that, in a silent embrace, for several minutes, before he eventually pulled away. She looked up into his eyes but could not read his expression. Raising her hand to his cheek, she tenderly stroked him and offered a small smile.

"Good night, Tam," she said softly as she took a step back.

He did not say anything, and she left him there in the library and went back upstairs to her room.

CHAPTER FIFTEEN

That morning

Tamworth did not sleep a wink that night and he suspected Sarah did not, either, judging by her tired look when they met at breakfast. They ate early—what was the point of lying in bed any longer?—and left the manor before the hour of seven.

Hardly any conversation eventuated over breakfast or in the carriage. Something had happened to him last night in the library; something he couldn't explain. Sarah had done something to his emotions, and he had been feeling lost ever since. She was very distant this morning; her responses measured and her expression shuttered. He couldn't read her, which was a first.

He dropped her at *La Robe Dorée* with the promise to return and fetch her in the evening, before proceeding to Paragon. He had not been to the club in more than two days and liked to visit all his premises regularly. When he arrived, there was a message for him from Rupert Belleville. His request had been fulfilled and Clara Hart had been located. She was staying at lodgings just outside of Boston. It would be an hour's ride from *La Robe Dorée* by his estimation. If he left now to pick Sarah up, they would be there in an hour and a half at most.

Tam had not yet removed his greatcoat, so he gathered up his hat from the desk and marched back out of the club to his carriage.

He arrived at Sarah's shop more quickly than expected and entered. It was very busy inside with at least seven women fluttering about. Once they became aware of his presence, however, all of them froze, then began to whisper. He did not care what gossip he attracted. He found Sarah and drew her away from the others.

"What is going on?" she asked, her face scanning his features. "It's not my sisters—"

"No. They are fine. Get your cloak, Sarah, we have found her. We need to leave immediately."

"I beg your pardon?"

"I will explain on the way," he threw over his shoulder as he stalked out of the shop.

Some minutes later, a very flustered Sarah joined him in the carriage. He did not wait for her to properly settle before he began to talk.

"Rupert Belleville is a friend, contrary to what I told you the other night. I don't know why I couldn't just admit that. But that is beside the point. I called in a favor and asked him also to search for Mrs. Hart. It was an alternative plan and it worked better than I expected. He has found her! Apparently, she is staying in lodgings just outside of town."

"How did he find her so fast when the police could not?"

"Do you think the police competent?" he asked wryly.

"Some of them are, but not all."

"Rupert worked for the military in a very…shall we say, clandestine capacity."

Sarah's brows rose.

"During his service, he built a network of informants and he maintains contact with many of them."

"That is impressive," she said. He wondered who she was impressed by—him, or Rupert? "He has never struck me as one who was into that sort of work."

Alas, she was impressed by Rupert.

"What should we do once we arrive at the lodgings?" she asked.

"I thought we would pretend we are guests. I tell you this now so you are not surprised later and decide to have me drawn and quartered." She raised her finely shaped brows in question. "We will pose as a married couple."

"I do not think that is a very good idea," she said immediately.

Tam knew she would argue, so he presented her with another alternative. "What else do you want us to pose as? Brother and sister?"

She went quiet then for a bit, until she said, "All

right. Anna and Penforth did that, when they were searching for Libby. If they can do it…"

Relief filled him. She would not fight this idea. "We will secure rooms and then we will find her." He leaned back, watching her. "What do you think?"

"It sounds like an all right plan, but I think it needs a little something more."

Surprise colored his voice when he said, "What do you suggest?"

"When we find her, I think you should distract her while I search her room for the necklace. She is unlikely to be wearing it, is she?"

He frowned. "How do you propose I distract her?"

Sarah shrugged. "I don't know. You are a man and most of the ladies of my acquaintance think you are a very handsome rake." She gave him a false smile. "You could use your rakish charm."

"Fine," he agreed. "Do *you* think I am a rake, though?"

She shrugged again. "What does it matter what I think?"

It mattered to him. A great deal.

"I don't believe you are," she said, after some time. "You are too brooding to be a rake. The ladies think you are because they do not know what to make of you. You appear to them as a mystery and they lack the boldness to solve you."

A wry smile curved his lips. "To *solve* me? But *you* have the courage to solve me, do you not?"

"I do have the courage, but unfortunately I have been unable to solve you."

Tam sat back, pondering what she had just said. There was a hidden meaning in her words but it eluded him.

SARAH WAS NERVOUS WHEN THEY ARRIVED AT THE lodgings, for several reasons. Everything was coming to a conclusion. She was finally going to pay off her father's debt and yet, at the same time, that would mean Tam would be out of her life.

This time, he would disappear forever, as he would want nothing more from her.

It would take some time to get back to a normal existence, but she believed she could do it. She had done it once before and could again. It was the pain in her heart she was not yet ready for, however.

She stepped down from the carriage and looked up at the red brick building in front of her. It seemed like a nice place and looked respectable. Had Mrs. Hart been hiding here for some time? If no one knew who she was, or the fact that she was wanted by the police—and the Raven—she could have been hiding in plain sight all this time.

Tam held out his arm and she took it. They needed to look like a happily married couple. Well, not *happily married*, but at least a married couple. The interior was much like the standard interior of any respectable lodgings, with a small desk in the front hall and people milling about, carrying on with their lives.

Sarah wondered what she would do if they ran into someone they knew. But the likelihood of that happening was small in a place such as this.

Tamworth approached the desk and rang the bell for service. "We would like your best suite of rooms, preferably separate rooms with connecting doors," he ordered.

Sarah appreciated his effort to respect her privacy by reserving separate rooms. Now that she thought about it, posing as a married couple was a good way to keep suspicion at bay. It wasn't as if she had a shiny white reputation to uphold. As much as the society ladies treated her as one of their own, the moment she lost her home and fortune and had to take a job, her reputation as a Boston elite had been tarnished. As a working woman, she was now different to the others, in their eyes. And in her own.

Still, she continued to hope they wouldn't see anyone they knew here at the lodgings. There was a difference between becoming a woman with a shop, and being found sharing a bedroom with the Raven!

They had no bag to be carried up to their rooms, so they simply climbed the stairs arm in arm, with Sarah making a show of being an adoring wife.

She could be an adoring wife in reality with the right man. But the right man was ostensibly the wrong man, and she did not want any other man.

"I am going downstairs to see what I can find out about Mrs. Hart," Tam said.

"Do you know what she looks like?"

"Yes." He nodded. "Will you stay here?"

"Do I have a choice?" she asked jokingly.

"No, my lady. You do not."

He left her to go information hunting and she sat in one of the chairs by the window and looked out into the courtyard below. It was a rather busy establishment, busier than she had first thought. While staring aimlessly, she caught sight of a woman who looked a lot like the one in the portrait she had been given. Was that Mrs. Hart? She was having a conversation with a man in the courtyard.

The woman finished her conversation and began to move toward the area where carriages were waiting. It appeared as though she was heading out somewhere. This would be a good time to search her room for the necklace. Tam would not even need to distract the woman. But then Sarah realized they did not know which room she occupied.

Mrs. Hart was now in a carriage and the man she had been speaking with was climbing up to the driver's seat.

Tam rushed into the room just then. "I saw her. She is leaving."

"Yes." She pointed out the window at the departing carriage. "But the problem is, we don't know which room she is in."

"We do. Rupert got that information for us." He

took her hand and pulled her along. Coincidentally, Mrs. Hart's room was just down the hall from their own suite.

Tam tried the door handle and found it locked. He reached into his coat pocket and pulled out a skeleton key.

"I am not going to ask what you are doing with a skeleton key, Tam."

"And I am not going to ask how you know what a skeleton key is," he said as he inserted the key into the lock. Within a second, the door opened and they stepped inside, closing it firmly behind them. Like their own chambers, the window in this room overlooked the courtyard. The first thing Sarah did was bolt to the window to see if Mrs. Hart had left. The carriage was still sitting there, though it appeared the driver was positioned to begin the ride.

"Start looking," she said to Tam. "I will keep watch."

Tam did not respond and when she glanced in his direction, she found him already searching the drawer beside the bed. How impressive, she thought, watching his movements for a moment. She turned back to the courtyard and saw the carriage begin to move but then it suddenly stopped and the door opened and the steps folded out. Mrs. Hart stepped down, lifted her skirts, and began to walk back into the building.

She sucked in her breath. "She is coming back, Tam!"

He looked up. "What?"

"She just exited the carriage and is coming back inside."

He cursed under his breath before straightening, and beckoned her to follow him out of the room. Once they were in the hallway, he said, "Go back into our rooms and I will try to distract her as you suggested when she comes up the stairs. Once I get her away, you can come back and search."

Sarah gave him a nod and turned swiftly to return to their rooms. There was a rush in her blood. It came from awareness of Tam, as much as it did from the potential danger of their situation.

She did not close the door behind her when she entered her room. She left it ajar slightly, and poked her head out a little so she could see what was going on.

Mrs. Hart appeared in the hallway and turned toward her room. She had her back to Sarah. Tam pretended he was walking toward the stairs and then stopped, looking at Mrs. Hart.

"Excuse me, Madam, are you Dora Warner?" he asked, using the name Rupert had told them she was using here. The woman stopped. Sarah could not see her face.

"Who is asking?" she said in a cold voice.

Tamworth smiled then. That debonaire smile of his. "I am Andrew Milton and I saw you at the bar yesterday evening."

"How do you know my name?"

"Oh, come now, Miss Warner. Don't tell me you do

not know the lengths a man will go to attain something that catches his interest."

Sarah clenched her teeth when she heard that and wished she had not suggested he use his rakish charm. Heavens, what had she done?

"Oh?" The woman's voice took on a sultry tone and she stepped closer to Tam. "Is that so?"

"Indeed." He smiled again and Mrs. Hart moved even closer to him and laced her arm through his.

"Mr. Milton. I was on my way out, but I forgot something and returned to fetch it. I suppose we are both very fortunate that I forgot that thing." She pointed at her room with her finger and leaned in to whisper something in Tamworth's ear.

He leered at her. "Why don't we go downstairs to the bar and have a drink first? The room will be there when we return. What do you think?" His voice was incredibly convincing.

If Sarah could put her jealousy aside, she could admit that he did well. But she still regretted her suggestion, despite the plan working perfectly.

With Mrs. Hart on his arm, Tam went downstairs. Sarah waited a minute or two before she quietly left their suite and crossed the hall to the woman's room. The door was still unlocked and she slipped inside.

She began with the drawer Tam had looked in earlier but found it empty of anything important. Then she proceeded to open every drawer she could find and still found nothing. The woman traveled very light, because there was not a bag with her belongings in sight. Sarah checked under the bed and found only speckles of dust.

She did find a bag in the dressing room, but there were no discoveries to be made as it contained only a dress and a small leather-bound book that appeared to be a journal.

Breathing hard from her exertion—she'd had to search as fast as she could and even crawl on her hands and knees—she placed her hands on her hips and surveyed the room. She was looking for anywhere that might be capable of hiding a necklace. Tam had told her that it was contained in a black velvet box. Unless she carried the box, which Sarah suspected was too big to fit inside a dress pocket or a reticule, then it had to be in this room. Unless, of course, she no longer had it at all.

Sarah returned to the dressing room and looked around a bit more. She opened the bag again looking for hidden compartments and still found nothing. She was about to return to the bedroom when she noticed the petticoats and crinoline on the floor. It had not occurred to her that something could be hidden beneath undergarments so casually thrown down, but as she stood there looking at the pile, she thought it the perfect place to hide something.

She hefted the garments and sure enough, there sat a black velvet box. She reached for it quickly and opened it to confirm there was a necklace inside. There was, but she didn't have time to study it, so she snapped the box shut and rushed back to her room in their suite.

She turned the key in the lock, driven by fear of discovery. When Tam returned, he would just have to enter through the door connecting her room to his.

A breath of relief gushed out from between her lips and she carried the box to the four-poster bed in the center of the room. Plopping down, she carefully opened the box, not in the manner she had earlier while in haste, but with delicateness this time.

The most brilliant ruby necklace lay exquisitely on velvet and she reached with one fingertip to touch the jewels. The rubies were heart-shaped and surrounded by small diamonds. She counted twenty-four of the red gems and did not bother with the diamonds. There were too many. This piece of jewelry must be priceless. And it was going to pay off her father's debt.

She lowered the lid of the box and lay down on her back, staring up at the bed canopy but not seeing anything in particular. She clutched the box to her chest. Tears stung the backs of her eyes at the finality of what would happen once Tamworth returned.

He would take the box and declare her debt paid in full. Then they would leave these rooms and he would drop her back at *La Robe Dorée*. He might return for her in the evening, or he might not. After she closed the shop, she would have to travel to Raven Hall and collect her sisters.

Once they were home, free of debt at last, their lives would change. Her earnings from *La Robe Dorée* would no longer go into debt payment and she could begin saving the rest. She would see Millie married to Jace

Campbell while she prepared Bella for her debut in five or six years. Yes, five years would be time enough to turn her sister into a proper lady.

But what would she do after Bella married? Retire to the country and embrace the charms of bucolic life?

For that matter, what would Tamworth Arbusson do after she gave him the necklace?

The door connecting her room to his opened just then and he stepped in, tall and dark, intimidating and brooding. Sarah sat up and held the box out to him. He came to stand in front of her, hesitating before he collected the box and opened it. She watched him carefully as his eyes appeared to scan every detail of the necklace. She could not guess what he was thinking at that moment.

"Tamworth," she said, when she felt too much silence had prevailed.

He looked at her then, his expression still unreadable. "It's done," he declared. "When we return to Boston, I will have a document drafted to indicate your payment is complete."

CHAPTER SIXTEEN

Several days later

The Smith-Jones girls returned to their home in South End. Millicent and Arabella were overjoyed, but Sarah was not. Although happy to have such a massive debt lifted from her shoulders, her heart was empty. And that emptiness grew with each passing moment.

Genteel poverty was behind them, it would seem, and promising nuptials were on the horizon, but if one looked deep, they would see a cut that was festering instead of healing. While there were many healers about, Sarah thought this cut could only be mended by the one who had made it.

Two days after she and Tam returned home with the necklace, he sent a messenger to *La Robe Dorée* with a document confirming her debt paid in full. Just as he had promised. She had secretly hoped that he might deliver the document in person.

How sentimental of her. How ridiculous of her.

Tam was not… No. She had to stop thinking of him as Tam.

Tamworth was not a man of sentiment.

Tonight, she was working late into the evening. *La Robe Dorée* had closed over two hours ago and Camilla had long departed for home. Sarah had sent word earlier to her sisters, informing them that she would not be home until after dinner.

The past few days had been difficult and Sarah still wasn't sleeping. She had immersed herself completely in her work in order to numb the ache in her heart. Her appetite was not what it should have been, but she hoped that would change for the better with time. When she had first fallen out with Tam a number of years ago, she had not been able to eat a bite for days. Slowly, her appetite had returned. It would return this time, too. Hopefully.

A knock sounded on the shop door just then, and she dropped the spool of thread in her hand and rushed to answer it, realizing she had been expecting Tam to show up at her door. She quickly turned the key in the lock and pulled open the door without looking first through the window.

Her heart leaped.

But not with joy.

A hulking giant of a man stormed past her into her shop and then hit her on the head with something blunt.

At first, she felt nothing but shock. Then her legs gave way beneath her and she crashed to the floor. Her vision blurred and a dull ache began in her head.

"Pick her up," a female voice commanded.

The voice sounded familiar… It was…

Sarah squeezed her eyes shut as the pain in her head intensified. That voice sounded like Mrs. Hart. But then, she could be imagining things, because of her injury. When one was laying down, horizontal, they often did not feel dizzy, but Sarah could feel the room spinning. *Was* it Mrs. Hart? Why didn't her eyes work? Why did she feel so…unwell?

And then everything went dark.

Paragon Club
The same evening

TAM HAD NOT BEEN ABLE TO CARRY OUT A SINGLE TASK that required mental energy since the day Regina's necklace had been recovered. After he had dropped Sarah back to *La Robe Dorée*, he had returned here to Paragon and summoned his solicitor to draft the document confirming the Smith-Jones debt repayment. Then he had sat staring into space, feeling empty, until it was time to collect Sarah and take her home to Raven Hall.

She had initially insisted on taking her sisters home that same day, but he had presented the argument that traveling in the late hours of the evening was not ideal for ladies. She had agreed and spent one last night at Raven Hall before leaving with her sisters very early the next day.

Tam had not left Raven Hall that day. He had roamed the halls of his now barren home, brooding and feeding the gloom inside of him. After the solicitor had prepared the document, he had ridden on horseback to deliver it to her in person. On arriving at the shop, he had stopped himself, and given it instead to a young man to deliver it, while he watched from the shadows to confirm she received it.

Every evening after that, he found himself loitering by her shop. This evening had been no exception. He had arrived around closing time and stood in the cold watching the place for an hour before finally returning to Paragon.

His steward knocked on his office door and he looked up with a beleaguered expression on his face. He had asked to be left alone.

"What is it?" he snapped. His temper had been short lately.

"A message for you, sir," his steward said. "The messenger said it was urgent."

He collected the note and unfolded it. He felt the blood drain from his face as he scanned the contents of the paper.

When Sarah came to her senses, she was seated on the floor, her hands bound behind her to the leg of a heavy settee. Her own settee. She was still in *La Robe Dorée*.

"You are awake. Good," Mrs. Hart said.

"*You*," Sarah rasped. Her throat was dry and she felt as if she were about to be violently ill. There was a throbbing in her head.

"Yes, me," Mrs. Hart replied. "You and the Raven tricked me. See, I made the mistake of not knowing what he looks like, and I allowed him to take me down for a drink at the lodgings, only for him to ditch me a moment later. When I returned to my room, my grandmother's necklace was missing. Good thing my man Duke saw the two of you leaving the lodgings and we tracked you down."

Sarah looked up at her, seeing what she looked like in person for the first time. She was a pretty woman, or had once been a pretty woman. There was a hardness in her eyes that reflected the hardness of her heart, and there were harsh lines at the corners of her mouth and eyes.

"That is not your grandmother's necklace," Sarah spat, trying to explore the binding to see if there was any chance to untangle herself.

"It doesn't matter whose necklace it was. It is *mine* and I am going to get it back. Now, I have sent word to your precious Raven to bring me the necklace in exchange for you."

Right! "I hate to tell you this, but that is a mistake. He will never come for me, much less exchange a necklace as valuable as that."

Tamworth had what he wanted. Regina's necklace, along with the memories it evoked, was the most precious thing in the world to him and he would not part with it for anything.

Sarah had to think fast of a way to extricate herself from this situation. She remembered seeing a man with Mrs. Hart earlier. He had been the one who had hit her. He was not here now and she had to take advantage.

"You are a madwoman," Sarah began; a tactic to distract her and rile up the woman. "First you kill your husband—"

"He tried to kill me first!" she shouted. "He made me believe he loved me, only to deceive me into marrying him and squandering my fortune."

"And you thought killing him was the answer?"

She shrugged and twisted her mouth. "Someone else would have killed him if I had not. Your Raven would likely have killed him."

That was not true. Her Raven would never take a life. She knew it with all her heart.

"Like I said, you are a madwoman. You took something that does not belong to you." She spotted a pair of small scissors under the dress she had been working on earlier. They were close to her but she could not reach them without her hands. Unless…

"I did not steal it. I inherited it. Nolan stole it and when he died it became mine."

"See? Nolan did do something good for you, after all."

"No, he did not!" She grew agitated just then and peeked out the window. "Where is Duke?"

"Is he the one you sent to tell the Raven to come get me?" Sarah asked. The woman had her back to Sarah and she quickly shifted position and bent her leg in such a way that she was able to kick the scissors toward her bound hands.

Mrs. Hart turned then. "Yes! Who else would I have sent?"

Sarah shrugged. "You will just have to let me go because no one is coming to exchange that necklace for me."

"Then I will simply kill you." Her eyes showed a murderous glint in them and Sarah's heart pounded in sudden fear.

She sucked in a quick breath and surreptitiously reached for the scissors. Somehow, she managed to get hold of them. She turned the blade against the fabric binding her and began to saw at it, carefully watching Mrs. Hart all the while. The woman was getting anxious.

Sarah knew the talk about killing her was not a threat. Mrs. Hart already had blood on her hands and would no doubt do it again without hesitation.

Mrs. Hart paced back and forth and then peered out the window yet again. Sarah's hands chose that moment to pop free of their binding. She jumped to her feet.

Ignoring the dizziness and pain in her head, she ran at Mrs. Hart.

"NATE..." TAM HEARD THE TREMOR IN HIS VOICE AS HE dropped the note from Mrs. Hart. Sarah was at her shop, tied up, and under threat of death.

He cleared his throat and tried again. "Get a carriage to this address." He scrawled Sarah's home address hurriedly on paper. If Sarah was a target, then her loved ones certainly were, too. "Go with the driver. Tell the butler, Cooper, that I sent you to retrieve Lady Millicent and Lady Arabella. Take Cooper and the housekeeper with them if you must. Get them all to Raven Hall. *Fast*!"

"Will do," Nate replied, taking the paper from Tam's hand and marching out of the room just as Paragon's steward, Coleman, walked in.

"Your carriage is ready, sir. And your horse, as you requested."

"Good. I'll ride ahead. Make sure the carriage gets to *La Robe Dorée* quickly." He would ride to Sarah's shop and have the second carriage follow him.

He rushed out of Paragon and mounted his waiting horse. He should never have left Sarah alone. He should have stayed longer tonight, watching over her as he had done so often recently. He had been foolish again. He had wanted to give her space to trust him before approaching her with his true intent, and in doing so, had placed her safety at risk.

Tam had never intended for Sarah to pay the previous Earl Waelcombe's debt. Well, not after that first visit to her aunt's house. He *had* visited her on that day to inform her of the debt and make arrangements for its repayment, but the moment he laid eyes on her, and perceived her pain and vulnerability, he knew he could not collect. Instead, Sarah had stolen his heart.

He had come up with a plan to gain her trust and confirm her romantic inclinations toward him, with the nebulous idea of perhaps even proposing marriage.

That had all gone horribly wrong. When Regina's necklace had gone missing, he had seen an opportunity to get close to Sarah again. And now, after retrieval of the necklace and cancellation of the debt, he had planned to take things slow in order to re-establish the trust he had broken all those years ago.

Tam cursed under his breath and pushed his horse faster along the streets. He had endangered her life by coming up with such a harebrained scheme. She had been right to be afraid in the beginning.

He arrived at *La Robe Dorée,* jumped down from his horse, and ran into the shop, his heart pounding in his chest.

The sight that greeted his eyes pulled him up short.

Sarah and Mrs. Hart were involved in a fisticuffs fight. Remarkably, it looked as if Sarah—his magnificent Sarah—was gaining the upper hand. He quickly raced forward and inserted himself between them.

The strips of taffeta near the leg of a settee caught his eyes at that moment and made him realize that Sarah had managed to free herself. What a remarkable woman. Mrs. Hart made to attack Sarah again and he pushed her back into a chair near the window and stood over her to stop her from getting up. He then pulled a velvet box out of his coat pocket and proffered it to her.

"Here is the necklace," he said. "Take it and get out!"

"*No!*" Before he could register what was happening, Sarah snatched the box from his grip and threw it. It skidded beneath the hem of an unfinished dress resting on a dress form. "She can't have it. It's yours, Tam!"

While Tam gaped at Sarah, Mrs. Hart dove past him, trying to get to the box. Sarah kicked her, destabilizing her long enough for Tam to drag her away from the dress.

While the three of them scuffled, a man stepped into the shop and pulled out a gun. He aimed it at Sarah. And fired.

He missed her, hitting Mrs. Hart instead.

Tam quickly pulled out his own revolver and aimed it at the man. Now they stood with guns pointed at each other.

"Sarah," Tam said slowly. He couldn't risk taking his eyes off the intruder to see where she was. "I need you to leave. Get out of here."

"If she moves, I will shoot," the hulking giant said. Tam realized this must be one of Mrs. Hart's henchmen.

"No, you will not. I rarely miss, and my revolver is aimed at your head. Besides, you have a Colt Single Action, and you have not reloaded. I will shoot you before you can get either of us." His eyes darted briefly to the side, in Sarah's direction. "Sarah, at my command, get out of here." She was standing close to the door that led to the back of the shop.

"I will not, Tam," she said firmly. "I will not leave you. You came here for me. You brought the *necklace*! I will not leave you."

His jaw tightened. He would allow the joy her words brought to take him later. Right now, he had to keep them both alive. Taking a steadying breath, he swiftly lowered his aim and fired. The henchman dropped his gun and crashed to the floor, clutching his bleeding leg.

Sarah rushed forward and snatched up the man's gun.

Tam moved to where Mrs. Hart was lying and checked her. She was dead. "Help me," he said to Sarah as he tucked his revolver away and grabbed one of the henchman's arms. She grabbed the other and together, they flipped the grunting man onto his stomach and tied his hands behind his back. He was in pain, yes, but Tam did not want to take any chances. In his experience, people could always fight through pain.

When they were done, he reached under the half-finished dress and collected the black velvet box, but as he turned, he saw Sarah drop to the floor.

"*Sarah*!" Tam sprinted across and immediately pressed his fingers to her neck just below her jaw to feel for a pulse. It was there, thankfully. She moved then and he heaved a sigh of relief. She had merely fainted. "Oh, God, Sarah," he rasped, emotion choking him. "I thought…" He couldn't finish.

"I…I'm fine," she said haltingly. "He hit me on the head earlier." She pointed to the bound man. "I confess, I do have rather a headache."

"I need to get you to safety." Tam gained his feet and scooped her up into his arms, carrying her out of the shop and to his carriage that had just arrived. He gently delivered her into it, made sure she was comfortable, then instructed the footman to remain and watch the prisoner until he could arrange for the police to arrive. He then had the driver take them to Raven Hall.

A murder had just occurred in Sarah's shop but he needed to get her to safety before returning to sort things out. He pulled her into his arms and cradled her the whole way home.

Four hours later

TAM MOUNTED HIS HORSE OUTSIDE *LA ROBE DORÉE*, keen to get back to Sarah at Raven Hall. After he had delivered her there earlier in the evening and handed her to her waiting sisters and the housekeeper, he had returned to the shop by carriage, and met with the police. After taking a statement from him, they took

Mrs. Hart's body away. Her henchman was arrested and taken away for medical treatment for his wound.

The shop would need to remain closed tomorrow. He had no doubt many curious people would turn up wanting to have a look, but he would ensure that it was sparkling clean and ready for Sarah to resume business, as soon as she was well enough to return.

Luckily his horse was well-rested, having remained tied up outside Sarah's shop. The ride home seemed extra-long and tedious but he held on. As soon as he arrived, he took the stairs two at a time to reach her room. He was about to open the door when someone cleared her throat. A little someone.

"She is sleeping and must not be disturbed," Bella said.

"But I need to see her," he said, in a pleading tone.

Bella shook her head. "She was hit on the head and the doctor said she has suffered a concussion and should be allowed to rest."

He smiled down at the girl. She was one of the most precocious and amusing people he'd ever met. "What are you doing awake at past one in the morning?"

"Guarding the halls, of course."

"Why do you want to guard the halls?"

"So you don't disturb Sarah. I knew you would want to keep vigil by her bed."

Clearly, Arabella was also very perceptive.

"All right," he conceded. "Why don't we make a deal? Allow me to see her just for a few minutes and then I will do anything you want."

Her blue eyes glowed bright in the dim hall. "Anything, you say?"

"Yes."

"Go and see her then."

Tam opened the door and stepped in. Millie was in the sitting area, reading. When she saw him, she pressed a finger to her lips, indicating for him to be quiet. He nodded, and crossed to the bedroom where Sarah lay asleep.

He lowered himself onto the bed beside her, careful not to make enough movement to rouse her. He sat looking at her for several minutes before heaving a sigh.

He loved her. It was as simple and as complicated as that. He had loved her for a very long time. She was his match in every way.

The week before he had approached her about Regina's necklace, he had seen her at a gala event. She had looked radiant, and he wanted to fall on his knees before her and ask her to be his.

Tam hoped that when she woke, she would be able to forgive him and accept him. If she couldn't accept him, then he would truly be lost.

Leaning forward, he pressed his lips gently to her forehead and let them linger for a moment before exiting the room. He gave Millie a nod on his way out and found Lady Arabella still in the hallway.

"You took too long," she scolded.

He shrugged. "I couldn't help myself."

She grinned.

"Now what is it you want me to do?"

"Take care of her," Bella said simply, but her words held so much gravity.

"I will," he agreed.

"All her life she has taken care of other people. It will be good for her to have someone who can take care of her, for a change."

He squatted down, so he could at least try to match her height. "I promise I will take care of Sarah," he repeated firmly.

She sighed contentedly. "Now I can go sleep," she declared.

He chuckled. "You were not really guarding these halls, were you?"

She shook her head. "No, I was waiting for you so I could ask you this."

Tam began to smile. The pain and anger that had stopped his heart from truly accepting love for so long, were being washed away.

"Good night, Bella."

"Good night, Tam."

He turned and headed toward the stairs.

"Oh, Tam!"

He swiveled around. "Yes?"

"Can I live with you and Sarah in this beautiful manor house?"

He laughed then. "Of course. My home is yours, Bella."

"Good."

CHAPTER SEVENTEEN

The following day

When Sarah awoke, her head felt so much better than it had the previous evening. Despite having a concussion—according to the doctor Tam's butler had fetched—she remembered almost everything that had happened.

Most importantly, she remembered how Tam had come for her. Her heart filled with warmth. He would never have done that if he hadn't cared for her. Her assumption had been wrong, and she had never been happier to be wrong.

She stretched beneath the warmth of the covers, a good feeling enveloping her. She felt a presence beside her and when she turned her head, she found Bella sleeping. She swiveled back to check the time on the clock and found a black jewelry box lying there.

She sat up, before picking up the box and opening it. Regina's rubies.

"It is very pretty," Bella sighed beside her.

Sarah smiled. "I thought you were sleeping."

"I was napping and now I am awake. It is past four in the afternoon." She yawned and stretched. "Tam gave me that this morning to keep for you. He said it is yours. I put it there so you would see it when you woke."

Sarah's heart jumped. *What did she mean*? The necklace was Tam's.

"Thank you, Arabella."

"You are most welcome, Sarah. How do you feel?"

"Much better."

"Good. I will fetch Tam now."

Before Sarah could stop her, she jumped off the bed and ran out of the room. Millie walked in then.

"How are you feeling?"

"I feel better. Just a little headache."

"You had a concussion. I'm glad you're feeling better now," her sister said, smiling and coming over to sit beside her on the bed.

"Is that the necklace?" she asked, pointing with her chin at the open box on Sarah's lap.

"Yes."

Millie's eyes widened. "It is very beautiful. Why did he ask Bella to give it to you? I thought it was his."

"I don't know," Sarah said, wondering.

"He really cares for you, you know. If only you had seen how frantic he was when he brought you home last night."

Sarah frowned. A lot had happened and there were definitely things she needed to know. "You were here when I was brought in?"

"Millie nodded. Tam sent a carriage to pick us all up, including Cooper and Mrs. Fowler. We were brought here to be kept safe."

Tam must have done that on receiving the news of Mrs. Hart holding her hostage. Her heart softened even more than it already had. He was a good man. She didn't care about what had happened between them in the past. He had proven himself worthy.

"Sarah!" Bella called from the sitting room. "I am announcing Tamworth!"

Millie burst out laughing. "That girl will make a good herald."

Sarah laughed too. "Send him in!" she called.

Tam walked in then, dressed immaculately as usual. Suddenly, she felt very self-conscious and pulled the covers up to her neck. She had just woken up and she was sure her face looked groggy and her hair matted to her skull.

"How are you, Sarah?" he asked in a tender tone.

"I feel much better."

"I am glad." He did not say anything more. He only stood there looking at her.

Still feeling awkward, she said, "May I dress?"

He seemed to realize her state just then. Color flooded his cheeks. "Of course. I only wanted to see how you were doing. I asked Bella to notify me as soon as you woke."

He looked at her sisters then. "Come, let's allow her some room."

They followed him out and a short while later, June came to help her bathe and dress. She donned a simple dress of sage green and lilac and chose not to add a corset to the mix. Today, she deserved time off any kind of binding whatsoever.

Instead of remaining in her room, she went downstairs. She was heading toward the dining room looking for food, when Tam found her.

"Should you really be out of bed?" he asked, a frown furrowing his eyebrows.

"I am restless," she admitted. "And hungry."

He covered the distance between them and took her hand. "I have that taken care of. Your food is ready but not in the dining room. I want you somewhere more comfortable." He led her to the library, and made her sit on one of the comfortable sofa chairs before leaving the room.

When he returned, he was carrying a tray of food. Her mouth dropped open.

"What are you doing, Tam?"

"What does it look like? I am bringing you food, of course." He set the tray down on a center table before coming to sit next to her. "What do you want to start with?" He reached over to uncover the dishes.

Sarah stayed his hand. "I want to talk to you about something first, before I eat," she said.

"What is it?"

"I found Regina's necklace in my room this morning. Bella said you gave it to me."

"Yes."

"What does that mean? I don't understand."

"It means it is now yours."

Her lips parted in astonishment. "What?"

"Sarah." He took both of her hand in his. "My feelings for you are more important than jewelry or money. I never intended for you to pay your father's debts. Years ago, when we first met, I wanted to offer you marriage but I made some mistakes. I sought another opportunity to regain your trust through this ridiculous idea to have you help me locate the necklace. I could have used Rupert Belleville for that, but I just thought…well, that is, I just wanted…you."

"Oh, Tam…"

"I am sorry I endangered you by involving you with Mrs. Hart."

She shook her head. "We got justice, Tam. For Libby, for Anna, and for everyone that woman hurt."

Tamworth reached out and stroked her cheek. She felt tears pool in her eyes and she decided to tell him what was deep in her heart.

"I love you, Tamworth," she said.

His eyes misted. Those keen emerald eyes that hardly showed any emotion, were now growing moist.

"I have always loved you, Sarah. I loved you back then, and I love you now. I believe I always will." He reached out and wiped away a tear that she did not realize had fallen until then.

"But my background," she said. "The scandal of my father's death. Do you want someone with a tainted past?"

"Don't be ridiculous, dear heart. Think of *my* reputation. I am the bastard son of a duke, after all." He gave her a wicked grin, and she laughed with him. "We are quite the pair, aren't we?" he added.

"Indeed, we are," she agreed.

He gently pulled her into his arms. "You have denied me a kiss for so long," he murmured. Sarah raised her face to his to show him she was now ready for his kiss and the promise it held. Pulling her tight, he touched his lips to hers. In the connection, she felt his love; his protection. In his kiss, she found the piece that had been missing from her life.

After a long moment of tenderness, he pulled away and reached into his coat pocket to pull something out. He clutched it in his hand, hiding it from her.

"I have a question to ask you. You are an unconventional woman, and I am far from conventional myself. So, I feel I should do this in an unconventional way." Tam opened his palm to reveal the golden dress brooch.

A gasp escaped her. "You still have it!"

"How could I let it go? The day I gave this to you, I wanted to make you a promise but back then I was afraid. I want to make you a promise now. Will you marry me, Lady Sarah?"

"Yes!" She threw her arms around his neck—her

still-aching head all but forgotten—and kissed him. "I will marry you, Tamworth Arbusson."

He pinned the brooch to her dress as he had done that night in *La Robe Dorée*. She was delighted. It was entirely appropriate that he had given her a golden engagement *dress*, rather than a ring. Now she could wear it and show the world her freedom.

"I have one more thing for you," he said.

"Tamworth, I don't think my heart can take anymore."

He laughed heartily. "Your heart can take it. I have faith in you."

"Out with it then. What is it?"

He waved expansively around. "Raven Hall."

She blinked.

"When I had it built, it was with us in mind. With *you* in mind."

Sarah folded herself back into his arms, quite overwhelmed.

"And the girls love it," he continued.

"Thank you, Tam."

"Thank *you*, Sarah."

He was giving her a home, and in return she would give him a family. One whose members all loved him from the first moment they met him. She couldn't imagine a more perfect day than this.

EPILOGUE

So it was that two of the Smith-Jones girls married before the year ended. Not on the same day, of course, but a week apart, with Millie marrying Jace first. Lady Arabella twice got to be a pretty ring bearer, a fact that delighted the young girl.

Sarah and Tam had a lengthy discussion about Regina's necklace, and they decided together that a bigger legacy to her memory could be created. They sold the jewels, and used the proceeds to set up a charitable trust from which they could assist gentlewomen left in dire straits. Sarah's own experience made her keen to let other ladies know that they didn't have to remain helpless in such situations, but with the right support, could find the strength within themselves to take control of their own lives.

Her friends, Anna and Libby, were utterly delighted when they heard the news. Their interest in women's suffrage was well-known, and it seemed that Sarah herself had become a prime example of the values for which their beloved movement was fighting.

Once the charity was established, Sarah's new husband made a generous donation that matched the value of the rubies that had founded it. Together, she and Tam showed the world that the circumstances of one's birth did not matter.

What did matter, was what one chose to do with the life they had been given.

Tam and Sarah truly were partners in life, in business, and in love.

The End

ALSO BY AVA ROSE

I hope you enjoyed this story in the *Boston Heiresses* series by Ava Rose.

If you would like to see where it all began, read Anna and Pen's story in

Not Quite a Duchess.

Then read on for Libby and Henry's story in

Not Quite a Baroness.

Want to read more from Ava Rose? Sign up for her reader newsletter and be notified whenever a new book becomes available:

https://mailchi.mp/7a18b8bbf7aa/ava-rose-newsletter

ABOUT THE AUTHOR

Ava Rose writes sweet and clean Victorian historical romance and gothic mystery. Her heroines are feisty and independent and her heroes brooding and swoon-worthy. When she's not writing, Ava looks after the family, pampers various cats, and tries to find a smidgen of time for her husband. She lives in Melbourne, Australia.

www.ingramcontent.com/pod-product-compliance
Lightning Source LLC
Chambersburg PA
CBHW020143120726
47903CB00007B/2391

* 9 7 8 0 6 4 8 4 0 4 5 5 2 *